THE TRANSFER

Dan Stevens

Copy Editor Vince Font
Cover design by Judith S. Design & Creativity
www.judithsdesign.com
Published by Glass Spider Publishing
www.glassspiderpublishing.com

To Jane and Kate—I love you more than words can express.

And to the Basque Country, which will forever be my tierra santa.

PROLOGUE

The first leg of our plan was nearly complete.

Creeping toward the city center, we noticed more activity than was normal this early in the morning. Otxoa (*oh-CHOH-uh*) and I, breathing heavily, slowed down to plan out how we would arrive surreptitiously.

"Just a few more streets," he said, doubled over from exhaustion.

"Seems a bit busy, don't you think?"

Otxoa nodded and squinted as he tried to catch his breath. "We have to be careful. Come on."

We rode our bikes slowly along the streets, inching closer to the target location. In the distance there was muffled yelling, accompanied by a flickering light accentuated by its stark contrast with the dark Basque sky.

A feeling of dread began to grow in the pit of my stomach. The closer we got, the more I worried about everything falling apart. We were so close now. We couldn't fail him. We could not fail *them*.

At about fifty yards, we spotted what would be the first of several heavy-duty vehicles. Some had *Ertzaintza* emblazoned on the sides; others *Guardia Civil.* This was not good. Did they know? How could they have known?

As we got closer to the scene, remaining mostly out of sight from any patrolling authorities, what we saw was jaw-dropping. The damage that had been done to the apartment building was incomprehensible. Why would this have happened?

The sun was rising, and we were beyond exhausted. "I'm hungry. I'm tired. I need a shower. Let's head back. We can try and sort this out later. There's nothing else we can do."

He didn't look happy about it, but he nodded in agreement knowing we had run into a brick wall. "Alright. Let's go."

I turned around to head back to the bikes. As I did so, however, Otxoa spun me around.

"Look!" he said, pointing toward the building. "They're removing debris. You see what they've got?"

I followed the trajectory of his finger and saw an Ertzaina carrying something out to the street. My eyes went wide when I realized what it was.

"It can't be. How did that survive the blast?"

Otxoa looked as stunned as I was. "I have no idea. It doesn't make sense. I—"

He cut himself off as he saw what they carried out of the wreckage next.

A body bag. Then another. Then another.

Neither of us could look away. I was certain Otxoa had the same sinking feeling I did; they had killed him. He had done so much to help, but they had killed him. Had he resisted? Had it been a mistake? All we could do was stand there watching in disbelief as they loaded the bags into the back of the van bound for the morgue.

Otxoa shook himself out of it first. "Let's go." Noticing that I hadn't moved, he repeated himself. "*¡Oye, Elder! ¡Vámonos!*"

I closed my eyes before I turned around, but I couldn't stop them from welling up. Otxoa looked to be in the same boat. We had failed. Time was up, and we had failed. There was nothing more we could do.

CHAPTER 1

"Why wouldn't he just call and let us know what the plan is? Why have us go to the office in Las Arenas? I don't understand. Keeping us together would mean the area gets washed in six weeks," Elder Otxoa managed to get out between bites of toast. "Two new Elders with no knowledge of the area doesn't exactly seem like a plan to me."

"Maybe he's just decided to take the advice he was given and send us home," I responded. Straightening my tie in the mirror and giving myself one last glance, I ran my fingers over the scar on the left side of my abdomen. It was still tender, and I winced in pain.

"You good?"

I nodded. "Look, I have no idea. Maybe he'll give it to the Hermanas."

"They'd be covering a lot of ground."

I half-smiled and briefly chuckled. "Hermana Maduro and Hermana Casillas could get it done, though. You could give them the whole city and they'd be just fine." He nodded in agreement. Shifting gears, I looked at Otxoa and, with a raise of the eyebrows, slightly inclined my head. "Your turn?"

"Yeah." We knelt by the front door of the *piso* and Otxoa offered a prayer before we left for the day. "He can't send us home," he said after he finished. "Not with one transfer left."

Silence hung in the air as we left and boarded the elevator. From the fourth floor, we descended to the lobby and waved to the doorman, Javier, who returned the greeting.

"Headed out to save Basque souls?" was his daily question.

"Basque or no . . . you first?" was our daily response.

Javier smiled and waved us off, like always. He had a young daughter with his now ex-wife, and apart from his job and his love of *fútbol*, he seemed to live a fairly solitary life. His habit of holding onto our letters and packages so that we were obligated to talk to him whenever we came in for lunch or at the end of the day was, at first, somewhat frustrating; however, we came to see it as endearing the more we got to know him.

The cold air rushed inward as we opened the doors to a rare, cloudless Basque sky. I looked up at the sky and couldn't help but remember that I was ninety-nine percent sure I'd once seen rain falling from a cloudless Galician sky. I instinctively checked for my umbrella. Noticing this, Otxoa looked at me and raised an eyebrow. He made it a point to look up at the sky and then back at me.

I shot him a quick glance and sighed. "You know how quickly it can change," I said, pausing slightly. "Wouldn't want to get caught in the rain."

Otxoa lowered his previously raised eyebrow and continued walking forward, solemnly, without responding.

Rounding the corner, he removed the cell phone from his pocket to check the time. "Missed call from Elders Ramos and Ortega. Probably wondering if we knew anything else about our mysterious trip to the mission office in Las Arenas." They had already learned that they'd be remaining together as companions for the next six-week transfer interval, as would the Hermanas.

"So nosy." I couldn't blame them, however. The routine was to expect a call from the mission president on the last weekend of the transfer if your area, assignment, or companion were going to change. No call meant no change. No such protocol existed for a face-to-face visit with the mission president at his office.

I knew the Church's leadership in Europe didn't necessarily agree with our decision to finish our mission, but Presidente Gonzalez had defended us and promised to closely monitor our physical and mental health. If it got bad enough, we'd be on the next flight home. We knew, however, that we had just six short weeks to make a mark. Six short weeks to justify not only our continued presence in the mission but, as we also felt, our very existence. It had to be meaningful. We had a debt to pay. An account to balance.

And time was running out.

Having spent much of the morning merely theorizing about the purpose of our visit, we picked up the pace to make up for lost time. It wasn't often that we used the Metro, as we could reach most places within our own area on foot; or, if we were really in a hurry, by bus. The Metro could be confusing for the uninitiated, but since our use of it mainly consisted of rare trips to Las Arenas, there wasn't too much to figure out.

Finally arriving at the station, we bought our passes and boarded. What could Presidente possibly want? What news awaited us? The anticipation was killing me.

The doors closed and the train began its acceleration toward the next stop. Shortly after taking our seats, Otxoa nudged me and pointed to the word *Askatasuna* written on the seat next to us. The two of us stared at the word as the train car swayed, hypnotically, back and forth . . .

Four Months Earlier:

"*Euskadi Ta Askatasuna?*"

Kemina got up from her seat and disappeared behind the bakery's counter to look for something. Returning to the table, she placed a newspaper in front of me and said, "It means 'Basque Homeland and Freedom' in Basque, or Euskera. It's what they call themselves. But they are more widely known as ETA."

I stopped chewing my *napolitana*. Living in Basque Country, it was impossible not to have heard about ETA, but I never knew the meaning behind its moniker. Not only had I seen the news reports of the bombings, but the Guardia Civil seemed virtually omnipresent. The headline of the newspaper read *Demonstration in San Sebastián Ends Violently as Calls for Release of ETA Prisoners Intensify.*

"Let me simplify things. These are the guys with the bombs," said Elder Otxoa.

"That's a bit of an oversimplification," responded Kemina, calmly.

Otxoa looked empowered. Directing his statements at Kemina, he said, "I grew up learning to avoid them and their demonstrations. Large, unruly crowds, signs with the mugshots of Etarras and demands for their release." He then turned to me. "We didn't speak out because we never knew when the next attack would come!"

Kemina nodded. "Their methods are very controversial, yes, and I disagree with those methods. But what they want isn't just the release of their comrades. It's independence. They believe Euskadi, or Basque Country, would be better off in the hands of the Basques. Makes sense, right? Who better to handle our affairs than us?"

I frowned in confusion. "Would it ever happen? Won't the attacks just make the government in Madrid even more resentful?"

"Yes, and they know that. However, you must understand the history of this place." Otxoa smiled, perked up, and gleefully took a bite of his *napolitana*.

"You mean before Franco?"

"I mean even before Columbus sailed to America," responded Kemina. "Over a thousand years ago, the Moors invaded Spain and fought their way north. Having conquered most of the peninsula, they set their sights on Basque Country. However, they were never able to conquer us. Our fighting spirit is unlike any other. We've never wanted *anyone* governing us *except* for us. When the Moors were finally expelled from the peninsula, there was a unification of different kingdoms. We were forced into this union, and for hundreds of years we've been forced to call ourselves something that we're not. In the thirties, a brutal civil war ravaged the country, pitting father against brother, cousin against cousin. After the Guerra Civil, Franco assumed power and saw us as a threat to his rule. He implemented strict rules about our language, culture, and freedoms. Some of my countrymen saw armed rebellion as the only option. After his death, they continued fighting, getting increasingly more violent as the years went on. Many here see it as a worthy cause."

Otxoa inclined his head toward Kemina. "What do *you* think?"

Kemina thought for a moment and took a deep breath. "I think . . . this isn't the way to get what one desires. It's not evil to desire independence or fight and stand up for what one believes. On the contrary, it gives one's life purpose, passion, fulfillment." Kemina looked down at her coffee. "But to do so in this manner, so violently and so recklessly without regard for innocent lives . . . I don't approve. And neither do most Basques."

I considered this for a moment. Kemina seemed different now, as if an old wound had been opened or a repressed memory had been brought to the forefront. There was a question I wanted to ask but decided against it. The wrinkles that raced across her forehead became more pronounced, and the veins in her hands, well-defined after a lifetime of hard work, bulged like they were looking to burst. Looking over at Otxoa, it seemed we shared the same train of thought. I shot him a look that implied it was better not to ask.

Kemina snapped out of it. Looking over at us, she smiled and said, "But not to worry. I'm sure they don't consider a couple of young men in white shirts and ties as enemies or threats."

We smiled sardonically. Looking at our phone, my companion realized it was time to go. "Well, Kemina, thank you for the *napolitana*, and for the history lesson."

Kemina smiled. "Anytime."

I was still seated, deep in thought about everything she had said. "Will it end?"

She closed her eyes briefly and shrugged before looking out the window at the rays of light that had forced their way through a group of departing clouds. "I don't know. Soon, I hope. You know how quickly the weather can change around here. Just try not to get caught in the rain."

Present Day:

. . . I awoke from my daydream as the train car slowed to a stop, the squealing of the brakes serving as the least desirable alarm clock I had ever had the displeasure of employing. Otxoa looked at me and shook his head. "You need to sleep more."

I nodded in agreement, still a bit groggy. "If only."

CHAPTER 2

Arriving at the office and buzzing in, we ascended to the fourth floor and walked to the front door. Pausing to compose myself before opening the door, I looked at Otxoa. "I'm not going home. I don't care if that's what this is about. I'm staying." He nodded in agreement.

We opened the door and walked into the foyer. The office Elders were the first to greet us. "Hey, Elders," said Elder Williams. "What's up?"

"Got called to the principal's office. Not sure why."

Elder Williams' companion, Elder Mendoza, answered. "It's got to be something to do with the transfer. It's probably time to send you guys home. You trunky yet? Anxious to get home?"

Otxoa rolled his eyes. "Mendoza, you know as well as I do that we've still got six weeks to go. But don't worry, because trunky or not, it'll leave me plenty of time to look up your sister in Barcelona while you're here scheduling bus trips and paying bills."

Mendoza grimaced and turned back to his work without

retort. Williams laughed. "You did tell me she's got a thing for big, burly Basque dudes." Turning his attention back to us, he said, "Have a seat, Elders. I'll let Presidente know you're here."

We sat down on the couch in the foyer and overheard Elder Williams teasing his companion about receiving a wedding invitation in the mail from his sister and soon-to-be brother-in-law, Otxoa. Mendoza tried to convince his companion that he wasn't worried about it, but he still had a year to go and wouldn't be able to do much about it from the mission office in Las Arenas. I'd seen enough missionaries go from fresh returned missionary to engaged in no time at all to know that, were I a betting man, it'd be a safe bet.

Our time spent waiting for Presidente meant I had a chance to look at some of the family photos hanging on the wall. I had met few people whose love for everyone was more genuine than his. Staring at the picture, I wondered if I still had those same genuine feelings after everything that had happened. I wondered if I could still make sense of my time here and find something to take home that filled the void in my heart, and not just a trinket to fill a void in my suitcase.

The door to Presidente's office opened and he came out to greet us. "Elders, thank you for coming. I'm sorry it was short notice." His Canary Island accent was welcoming and jovial. It was extremely distinct from the harsher Basque accent. He gestured for us to enter his office, so we entered and sat down.

"So, Elders, how have you been holding up since . . . ?"

Otxoa was the first to respond. "We're doing alright, about as well as can be expected, I think. No real complications."

I did my best to put on a poker face and confirm what Otxoa had said. Clearing my throat, I said, as convincingly as possible, "Yeah, fine, doing . . . well. Just . . . one day at a time, right?"

Presidente looked at me with some concern. "You know, Elder, there's no shame in admitting that it's been difficult. What you went through . . . not everyone experiences something like that. No one can expect to come out on the other side physically, mentally, or spiritually unscathed. I think the true test of a man's strength is admitting when he needs help."

Otxoa looked at me quickly out of the corner of his eye and again interjected. "Look, Presidente, I don't want you to worry about us. Really, we're doing okay. We're just eager to take advantage of the time we have left."

Gonzalez smiled. "That's very admirable, Elder Otxoa. I was hoping you would say that." His cell phone chimed and he looked at the screen. He raised his eyebrows and took a deep breath. "Excuse me," he said. He stood up from his chair and went to speak with Elders Williams and Mendoza. "Elders, why don't you go pick up some bread, cookies, and *Cola-Cao* mix for later."

Looking at each other, they shrugged their shoulders. "You don't have to tell me twice," said Elder Mendoza. They grabbed their things and left.

After making sure they were gone, Presidente Gonzalez again entered his office and sat down. He picked up his cell phone and shot off a message. Replacing the phone on his desk, he offered an apology. "I'm sorry to interrupt our conversation like that. It was urgent."

"No problem," I said, eager to talk about something, anything else.

He shifted gears and asked me a question. "Tell me, Elder. In your time here, what have you learned about Basque Country?"

I looked at Otxoa, who returned my gaze, one eyebrow raised, anxious to know how much I had actually absorbed. I recounted everything I knew.

"I must say, that's quite impressive. Rarely does an American missionary know more than the fact that Euskera is a difficult language to learn. I can see you love this place very much." He paused for a moment before dividing his attention between us equally. "Elders, how would you like the opportunity to make things right?"

I shot a skeptical look Presidente's way. "What do you mean? Like, revenge?"

Otxoa, surprised, chimed in. "I won't lie. It's crossed our minds once or twice. We know we shouldn't want it. But we just can't help it."

Presidente Gonzalez nodded and leaned back in his chair, considering what my companion had said. Feeling sheepish, we remained silent. He took pity on us and continued. "Revenge, Elders, is not what I'm talking about. I'm talking about introducing balance, or the possibility of it. I'm talking about restoring harmony. I'm talking about justice."

Otxoa and I jumped in our seats when we heard the door open to reveal a tall, dark-haired woman dressed in a business-casual manner and carrying a nondescript messenger bag. She confidently strode in and made her way toward us.

Presidente stood up. "Elders, this is Capitana Martinez.

We go way back."

Martinez extended her hand to each of us in turn, and we stood up to shake it. I sensed by her demeanor that she wasn't here on a social call.

"She's here to help us obtain that justice."

CHAPTER 3

"Your presidente, Juan Pablo, tells me you two have been here for some time."

Elder Otxoa responded, wary of the visitor. "Yes. We know the area."

Capitana Martinez raised her eyebrows as she read Otxoa's name tag. "Otxoa, eh? Well, this works out nicely."

I spoke up. "Who are you?"

She shot a glance at Presidente before returning her gaze my way. "I am a servant of the people of Spain. I work to protect them. I've come to Basque Country with a mission. Sort of like you two."

Otxoa's countenance changed noticeably. "Guardia Civil," he said, a sour look on his face.

Martinez walked over to the other desk in the office and leaned against it, crossing her arms. It was then when I caught a flash of a badge and a sidearm tucked away beneath her jacket. "Yes, Otxoa, Guardia Civil. Are we not also servants?"

"Servants?" he said with a sarcastic tone. "I suppose everyone serves someone."

She smiled wryly. "Yes, I understand, given our history up here, how you must feel about us. We've worked hard to project a more palatable version of ourselves over the years. I also serve as the Guardia Civil's liaison to Interpol, which, like us, has a vested interest in serving your countrymen." Standing up and stroking her chin, she continued, "But I think the question you should ask yourself is why am *I* here, and not your Ertzaintza?"

Otxoa looked at Presidente, then back at Martinez. "You're here because of what happened. You're not going to fill them in?"

Martinez shook her head. "The Spanish government doesn't allow the Ertzaintza to access Interpol's intelligence network. While a capable police force, there's too much of a risk of ETA infiltration. The gloves are coming off now, and there aren't many we can trust."

I began to feel very uneasy. What did Interpol and the Guardia Civil want with us?

Presidente Gonzalez interjected. "Elders . . ." he hesitated, moving forward in his chair and placing his hands on his desk while interlacing his fingers, "Patricia . . . eh, Capitana Martinez is here to help us, like I said." He looked directly at Otxoa. "She is not the enemy."

Martinez reached into her bag and retrieved a tablet. "Elders, have you ever heard the name Amalur Arzamendia-Kareaga?"

Otxoa laughed. "What, not going to recite all eight Basque surnames?"

The capitana shook her head, and without changing her expression, said, "Not necessary. We just refer to her as simply Heriotza."

Otxoa stopped laughing and quickly closed his mouth. The color drained from his face. He sat forward, placing his interlaced hands underneath his nose.

I looked over at him. "Heriotza?"

"Death," Capitana Martinez replied. Looking at Otxoa, she said, "That name, Elder, I'm sure you know." Pausing briefly before continuing, she said, "We believe she's the one responsible."

My blood ran cold. Out of the corner of my eye, I saw Otxoa grow even more tense. "What's prevented you from arresting her?" I asked.

Martinez handed the tablet to us. The photo on the screen was of a young, gorgeous Basque woman with long, chestnut-colored hair adorned with one solitary braid. Her nose was pierced on the left side, and she sported a tattoo of a bear painted red, white, and green on her right forearm. Her most striking feature, however, were her eyes. Her dark-brown eyes were deep and penetrating, so much so that they caused a shiver to run up my spine.

"Because," Martinez said, "until very recently, we haven't been able to directly connect her. We believe she's calling the shots, but she does a hell of a job keeping her name out of it. Most of the information we have on her has actually come to us recently." She paused, looking at each of us in turn. "Within the last four weeks."

I started to connect the dots. "How? What changed?"

"Someone has volunteered to help us. Someone with knowledge of the inner workings of ETA. My contact reached out to us shortly after the incident, and we've been trying to find the best way to communicate ever since."

I found myself nodding unconsciously. "You want us to be the go-between."

"Correct. You routinely walk the streets, striking up conversations with anyone and everyone. No one would suspect you're involved. All you'd need to do is meet with my contact under the guise of your missionary work, collect the information, and pass it on to us."

We looked at Presidente. "Is this okay? Have you already run it up the chain?"

"It took some convincing, but it's all squared away. I told them that until this ends, not even the missionaries will be safe." He stood up and walked over to Martinez. Looking at her, he said sternly, "Capitana Martinez has assured me that your safety will be their utmost priority. If we get even a hint that you're in danger, we'll pull you out." Turning toward us, he offered, "However, whether or not you agree to participate is entirely your decision. Neither I nor anyone else, including Capitana Martinez, will pressure you into volunteering."

"But make no mistake," said Martinez, slowly, through gritted teeth, "this is very important to me." Turning to look Otxoa in the eye, she continued, "Fear and violence have reigned here for too long. Too many families have been destroyed." She looked away as her eyes became red and misty. "Too many lives have been lost. We . . . *I* . . . have to end this."

I was hesitant to decide so quickly, and even more hesitant to decide in Martinez's presence. I needed more time, more information. "We need the room."

"Of course." Martinez cleared her throat in an effort to

compose herself. She looked at Presidente out of the corner of her eye on her way out. "I'll be right outside."

After she left, the three of us sat in silence for a few moments; I decided to break it. "We only have one transfer left. What if this goes on for longer than six weeks?"

"Well," said Presidente, "part of the agreement with the Guardia Civil is that our part in this operation ends when the transfer does. They know they've got a ticking clock if you two get involved."

I looked over at Otxoa, who had been uncharacteristically silent. "You're not going to say anything?"

He sat up. "*Mira*, Capitana Martinez came here because she knows what we know, I mean, deep down. Things are worse here than they've been in a long time." Otxoa furrowed his brow and paused. Looking up at Presidente Gonzalez and me, he said, "Heriotza . . . I've heard that name before. A few times. And that awful, sinking feeling we had when Martinez uttered it . . . it's not the first time I've experienced it. This idea may seem crazy, but it's never been done before, and I have to agree with her. I'll volunteer."

Presidente flashed Otxoa a quick smile before looking at me. "Elder, look, just because your companion feels this way doesn't mean you're obligated to do this. It's a lot to ask."

I wanted to feel hesitant. I wanted to find a way to poke a hole in this plan. But as much as I tried, as much as I wanted to say no, I couldn't bring myself to do so. I knew deep down, like Otxoa had said, that this was what we had been waiting for.

I stood up and looked at the two of them before walking to the door. I opened it and saw Martinez turn around to face me, arms crossed and eyebrows raised, obviously expecting an answer. "Capitana . . ."

She cut me off. "I know. Let's get to work."

Otxoa hit the button to call the elevator. "Well, I never had a class about *this* in the MTC. You?"

I chuckled. "Yeah. Week three during my training in the Missionary Training Center in Utah: 'Tradecraft in the Mission Field.' "

Our walk back to the Metro station was quiet, but what could be said? This territory was completely uncharted. Boarding the Metro, I began to feel like everyone else in the car was staring at us. Granted, this was normal; but I was paranoid now. There was no way they could know what our new assignment was, right?

The car began to sway back and forth, mirroring my growing ambivalence about what we had agreed to do. Did we act too quickly? Were we qualified to do this? All we needed to do was essentially the same thing we did every day: talk to someone on the street, share a thought, and report back on the progress.

"I can't wait to meet the contact and get started." Otxoa could hardly sit still, he was so excited.

"Whoever it is, I wonder if they'll get a free pass when this is over. I mean, they've got to be ETA if it's worth our undertaking something of this magnitude."

"Yeah, I'm not too worried about that. They'll get what they deserve. I only worry about Martinez's closeness to the case. She seemed to care much more than a typical Guardia

Civil, especially in this part of the country."

"I was thinking the same thing. I hope we're not in over our heads here."

Otxoa scoffed. "This is Euskadi. This is my home. If anything, ETA's in over their heads now that we're involved. It's like that phrase in English, 'Come at me, bro!'" I laughed and nodded. Otxoa smiled and looked off into the distance through the window. His tone more somber now, he said, "For Kemina."

I nodded again. "For Kemina."

CHAPTER 4

The rendezvous was scheduled to take place behind the Guggenheim Museum. Otxoa and I were to arrive at 18:00 hours and begin the ruse by speaking with a few people at random. After a half-dozen of the inevitable "I'm in a hurry" accompanied by a tapping of the wrist, or an outstretched index finger wagging back and forth while making a "tsk-tsk" sound, we figured we'd made enough attempts to avoid arousing the suspicion of anyone who may have been watching.

Martinez told us the contact would be standing by the estuary, facing north, near the Maman, a sculpture of a giant spider located behind the museum, and that we'd recognize this person by their green scarf.

The clouds that had been gathering above us finally decided it was time to let loose. Otxoa and I opened our umbrellas and continued forward, undaunted. As we made our way to the sculpture, he quietly recited the phrase we had been instructed to give the contact. Not only did we need to identify ourselves using the phrase, but Capitana Martinez wanted us to understand that this was how we'd be operating for the next six weeks. Psychologically, we needed to know we were all-in. She said that until we had uttered this phrase, the operation had yet to begin. For the contact, it was a way of knowing that we could be trusted to put everything we had into the endeavor, for which the contact was risking their life.

Approaching the massive spider, we spotted an individual in a green scarf. A shot of adrenaline coursed through my veins with each step, the reality of the operation sinking in. My legs were *flan* as we approached the contact, now less than twenty-five yards away. Struggling to take each step, we nevertheless made progress. Twenty yards, fifteen, ten, five . . .

We could now see that the contact was a young man in his twenties. He was slender, with black hair, bright blue eyes, and a clean-shaven face. He seemed uncannily familiar to me. I had an uneasy feeling, like when you're trying to remember something that's right on the tip of your tongue. Taking a deep breath, I composed myself. Otxoa must have been doing the same, since his face looked as determined as I'd ever seen it.

We finally arrived, and as we stood next to the contact, Otxoa removed a pamphlet from his bag and opened his mouth to speak. "*Arrotz-herri, otso-herri* (a foreign land is a land of wolves)," he said in Euskera.

Turning to look at us curiously, the man took the pamphlet from Otxoa's outstretched hand and replied in Euskera. "*Egia da latz eta garratz* (the truth is bitter and unpleasant)." He sized us up. "So, you're them," he said, switching to Castellano. He seemed unimpressed. "I take it you've been briefed?"

"We know what we're doing," said Otxoa.

The contact seemed amused by this. "Do you? Well, you've got confidence. And to volunteer to do what you're doing takes guts. Tell me, how is the good capitana?"

"Eager to get started, like us. What do we call you?"

The contact hesitated before making a "tsk" sound and looking away. "First, I want to know why you agreed to do this."

I began to get irritated. "Really? Is this how it's going to be?"

"Look, there's a lot on the line and I don't know anything about you two. A *zipaio* and a *guiri* have been entrusted to get this done. And in just six weeks! I need to know that I can trust you and that this won't be something you decide a few days from now is going to be too hard."

I looked at Otxoa. *"Guiri?"*

"You're a foreigner," he said, his jaw clenched. "And I'm a traitor."

I took a deep breath and realized it did us no good to start off on the wrong foot. "Otxoa is from San Sebastián. He's seen too much of what ETA can do. I've lived here for a while and have seen way more than I bargained for. These people deserve better. *You* deserve better." I looked at Otxoa, then back at the contact. "We lost a good friend, and we don't want their death to be meaningless."

Otxoa spoke up, still smarting about the *zipaio* remark. "You want to question our commitment? Fine. But remember one thing. *I've* never betrayed my countrymen. Can you say the same thing? How many Basques have *you* killed? How many families have *you* destroyed? And for what? An independent Euskadi? Are you really foolish enough to think that would end up happening? And if that's the case, why should we trust you?"

The contact raised his head slightly, then looked down and nodded. He turned his gaze to the estuary and walked to the railing. Staring contemplatively at the calm water below, he said, "Xabi (*CHAH-bee*). Call me Xabi."

"I think we want the same thing, Xabi," I said, trying to play the diplomat. "We want justice."

Xabi looked like he was pondering this. "How much did Capitana Martinez tell you about me?"

"Only that you recently returned from abroad and it seems like you've grown a conscience," said Otxoa defiantly.

Xabi looked at Otxoa, a smile slowly forming. "Then you don't really know anything about me. Just like I don't know anything about you. So the only thing we can do is decide to trust each other. And you're right. We do want the same thing."

"Can you meet tomorrow?"

Xabi pulled out a cigarette and lit up. "Well, it's not like I'm going to be starting a novel any time soon. I've cleared my schedule for this. You can come by the *piso* at 10:00."

I was surprised. "You don't want to meet outdoors?"

"Looks better if we do it at my *piso*. Looks like we have nothing to hide."

I slowly nodded. I wasn't sure whether to broach the topic of the operation's target yet or not. I wasn't even sure whether or not I was supposed to say her name. "Should we expect any other . . . guests?"

"No, she won't be there," Xabi said, blowing smoke into

the air. "She's not in town right now. But it needs to be expected that she or anyone else could be there at any time. Ring the *timbre* three times. If the coast is clear, I'll respond with two buzzes, one short and one long."

He turned to face us, shaking his head. "Martinez really told you to use that phrase to make contact with me, huh?" Otxoa nodded. "Well," Xabi said, preparing to leave, "make sure you talk to a few more people before you head back. It'll look more authentic. I'll see you tomorrow." He walked away and disappeared.

We stood at the railing, staring at the estuary in an attempt to process the conversation. Otxoa was leaning forward, resting his arms on the railing. After a minute, he stood up and slapped the railing. "We're in it now, man. Start the clock."

CHAPTER 5

Barakaldo was well outside of our area and quite the jaunt from our *piso*. In fact, it was deep in Hermana territory. We needed to make sure we stayed out of sight as much as possible, not only because we were sure to catch hell from the Hermanas at our weekly district meeting, but because the more people who caught wind of white shirts and ties hanging around the building, the more unwanted attention we would draw, which we could not afford.

Looking nervously at the clouds above, I rolled my eyes and hailed a taxi to take us from our building to Xabi's building in Barakaldo, saving us an hour and a half of walking. After paying the driver, we got out of the cab and walked up to the front door, quickly scanning the area to make sure no one would be able to recognize us.

"3D," said Otxoa.

I rang the *timbre* three times, pausing distinctly between each one, as we had been instructed. Xabi responded by pressing the buzzer twice, making sure the second time was elongated to let us know the coast was clear.

Entering the lobby, we greeted the doorman, who stood up, obviously wary of the two Mormon missionaries who had just entered the building. Surely, he must have thought we had done so under false pretenses, but he didn't seem like he was in the mood to challenge us, so he eyed us all the way to the elevator. We pretended not to notice and ascended to the third floor.

Walking up to D, we stopped and pressed our ears to the door. I could hear the TV. "I think we're clear," I said and knocked.

Xabi muted the TV and opened the door. "*Ongi etorri* (welcome). Thirsty?"

I refused, but Otxoa nodded. "Water, please."

"Something a little stronger?"

"Water will be fine."

Xabi shrugged and went to get the water. Otxoa and I found seats on a couch adjacent to Xabi's chair. Looking around the *piso*, I noticed the walls were bare; no photos, no shelves, nothing. Well, almost nothing. I wasn't sure if it belonged to him or if it was just property of the building owner, but there was a painting of a man and a boy on a boat in the middle of what looked like a lake. The color palette was so striking that I couldn't pull my eyes away. A golden glow of sunlight careened off of a brilliant blue lake, surrounded by trees so green they nearly burst.

Otxoa, however, wasted no time. "So, how long have you been back in Bilbao, and how did you find a place so quickly?"

Xabi looked back at us for a moment from the kitchen before returning his attention to the drinks. "Been back about three weeks. Some friends of mine own it. The previous tenants had to leave quickly and attend to some pressing business."

Otxoa looked at me and shoveled a load of imaginary bull droppings over his shoulder.

"It looks like you haven't quite moved in," I said. He seemed to be living out of his suitcase. "Not planning on staying long?"

Xabi laughed. "Don't like the idea of roots. You never know when you'll have to—"

"—leave quickly and attend to some pressing business?" said Otxoa sarcastically, finishing the sentence. Xabi shot a sardonic look Otxoa's way but otherwise ignored the quip.

I glanced at Otxoa and cleared my throat. "I thought about our conversation yesterday, and I've been thinking a lot about what's happened around here recently. And you were right when you said that we don't know each other and that we need to trust each other. Why don't you start by telling us about yourself?"

He looked at us for a moment, skeptically. His eyes darted back and forth between Otxoa and me, seemingly weighing whether or not to let down his guard. "I suppose you're right." He gestured toward the empty wall. "As you can see, I'm a sentimental guy. The plethora of photos of my friends and loved ones is evidence of that."

I didn't take the bait. "Tell us about them."

He clenched his jaw twice before continuing. "My 'friends' spend their days and nights fighting for an independent Euskadi."

Otxoa spoke up. "What about your family?"

Xabi walked to a suitcase sitting in the corner. Opening it

up, he pulled out a small box. "All I know about my father fits in here."

"I thought you weren't very sentimental."

Xabi tossed me the box. I opened it, and a wave of sadness overtook me before I passed it to Otxoa. "This is all?"

Xabi nodded and reached back into the suitcase to pull out what looked like a photo. I couldn't see it, but he stared at it for a moment. "That's what she told me. It was all she had to remember him by after he left."

"Is that your mother? Where is she now?"

He continued looking at the photo, ignoring the question. After a moment, he looked at Otxoa. "¿San Sebastián?"

"*Puro Vasco* (pure Basque)," said Otxoa.

Xabi replaced the photo and took the box from Otxoa and removed its lone contents: a pendant. He held it up, studying it longingly. "St. Ignacio. Never been religious. But I never had the heart to throw it out. It always did seem to bring me comfort."

I knew I needed to tread carefully. "Do your 'friends' bring you comfort?"

Xabi studied the pendant for a moment longer before returning it to the box. "Do yours?" he said, gesturing to Otxoa.

Where I was sensitive to the diplomatic angle, Otxoa was unsympathetic. "Why'd you join?"

He looked at Otxoa for a moment. "What would you like to hear? If you want, I can spin you some tale of romanticism involving a young, impressionable man who got swept up in talk of revolution."

"You're zealots, not revolutionaries."

"Well, we learned from the best."

Otxoa just stared at him. "What would your mother think?"

"My mother has nothing to do with this."

"Are you sure? Because you didn't offer to show us her photo. And you dodged the question about where she is now. What would she think of the terrorist she raised?"

Xabi walked over to Otxoa, who stood up to meet him. The clouds crashed together as the first bout of thunder rocked the sky above. My anxiety shot through the roof, but I couldn't let the operation sour on day one. "We're only trying to help. The more we know about you, the better we can operate."

Seemingly convinced, Xabi relented. "Alright," he said, taking a deep breath and relaxing before he continued. "I was on holiday outside of the country. Sitting outside of a restaurant and talking on the phone, I was approached by a woman who then sat down at my table. She didn't say anything until I finished my call, but I had decided to finish it early because she was so captivating. Once I hung up, she spoke to me in Euskera, having overheard me speaking it. She proceeded to flatter me and then invited me to an event she was going to host that night with some friends. I couldn't pass up an opportunity like that, so I agreed, and she gave me the details. She told me her name was Amalur."

Xabi squinted as he recalled the details.

"When I got to the building that evening, I could sense that I may have been in over my head. I was greeted by other people my age, all speaking Euskera, but in various dialects. They were welcoming, and we communicated with each other as best we could. After about ten minutes, she arrived. It became clear she was the leader of what turned out to be a special recruiting cell of ETA. She had a way with words like no one I had ever met. She was breathtaking; the way she walked and spoke . . . I was mesmerized. The feeling I had earlier of being in over my head had disappeared and I felt . . . enlightened, for the first time in my life. She spoke of freedom, of patriotism, of oppression, of the importance of the Fatherland. I was converted. Plain and simple. After she finished her speech, she spotted me and thanked me for coming. I probably seemed like a stuttering idiot. But in that moment, I was hooked. And she was the drug."

"Go on," said Otxoa, a hint of anticipation in his voice.

Xabi closed his eyes for a moment before slowly opening them. "Not long after that, I left my life behind, got acquainted with other senior members of the cell, and was eventually transferred to another location. At first, they fed me propaganda and brought me to protests. Fairly innocent stuff. I knew that the group was responsible for other, less innocent things, but I was on such a high that I decided to look the other way."

He stood up and walked to another corner of the room. Pausing before turning back to face us, he said, "Until one day when they asked me to train in explosives. I was hesitant, and they could sense it. They told me I wouldn't be harming anyone, that the bombs were for show. They would be used to send a message, but not for killings. Amalur even visited me. I was convinced, so I agreed and began my training. But it didn't quite go the way they'd promised."

He continued staring at us, but his gaze turned into a

thousand-yard stare. He began to stare through us, not just at us. Snapping out of his trance, he took a deep breath and sat back down. The silence between us was deafening. The weight this man held on his shoulders was immense, and I was hesitant to pry any further.

My companion, overlooking the disdain he felt for Xabi, sympathetically asked, "How did you get in contact with Martinez?"

"I contacted the Guardia Civil, anonymously, to tell them I had information that would be useful. Next thing I knew, I was dealing with Capitana Martinez. Apparently, she's the one they've tasked to assist with Interpol and, as an extension, ETA and Euskadi."

My anxiety began to rise. I started to sweat, and my vision became blurry. "Do you mind if I get some water?" I managed to say.

Xabi gestured to the kitchen with his head. Walking into the kitchen, I attempted to get my bearings and stave off an impending attack. A familiar yet unwelcome odor assaulted my sense of smell, and I noticed a pile of uncut garlic next to the sink. The attack was inevitable now.

Staying out of sight, I turned on the faucet, placed both hands on the sink, and took a deep breath. Closing my eyes, I saw chaos coupled with bodies and first responders. I smelled fire, heard the grim descriptions of the scene given by the firemen on site, and tasted the dirt lingering in the air. My skin hurt so much I wanted to shed it. This assault on my senses culminated in the form of a hellish, inescapable fear nestled in the pit of my stomach. Slowly, I began to list my surroundings, forcing the fear to retreat.

Otxoa came in to check on me. "*¿Todo bien?*"

I nodded, drank some water, and returned to my seat. Getting an idea, I said, "Xabi, normally when we visit someone for the first time, we have an introductory message. However, I'd like to share something different with you."

He gestured for me to continue.

"It's obvious to me that you've had to make a lot of difficult choices recently. Elder Otxoa and I will probably never know how hard they've been and what they may have cost you. We don't want to pretend to know who you are, what you've been through, or how you've somehow mustered the strength to leave all that you know to truly serve your countrymen."

"Serve?" he retorted. He looked at Otxoa as if to either bait him into another argument or—and I hoped this was the case—gain his approval. Otxoa was, after all, a fellow Basque. The first time we'd met him, Xabi had considered my companion a traitor. It was instinctive, sure, but I knew there had to be some complex feelings buried deep down that were beginning to rise to the surface.

I continued. "We volunteered to serve as missionaries. Because we chose to do this, we were assigned to Northern Spain; we didn't ask to come here. I've thought a lot about why this happened. I feel compelled to say that it wasn't at random, but the more I think about it, the more I question the 'why.' The fact is, though, we made a choice. Could things have gone differently? Maybe. Yeah, probably. But you made the same choice that we did. You chose to leave your home, to follow your heart, and to serve by meeting with us and working together. Why? I haven't gotten an answer yet, but there's no shame in that."

Xabi calmly returned my gaze, but I could tell the gears inside his head were spinning and that he was again deciding whether or not to lower his defenses. I hoped that we were breaking through. He pursed his lips as he looked at me then turned his attention to a silent Otxoa, who looked unsure if he should add something.

Finally, Xabi responded. "If you could go back and do it all again, would you make different choices?"

I shrugged. "Would you?"

He looked down. Then he looked back up at us, alternating between Otxoa and me. "Ask me again in six weeks."

CHAPTER 6

Leaving Xabi's building, I safely secured the information he gave us in a hidden compartment in the bag Martinez had provided us. I looked at Otxoa to gauge how he was doing and could sense he had a lot on his mind.

"Things got a bit tense in there, don't you think?" I said.

He didn't respond, but the look on his face said it all.

We made our way by bus toward the church to get to our district meeting, traveling mostly in silence. I weighed whether or not to press the issue with him but ultimately decided to do so. "What's up?"

After a moment, he let out an annoyed breath. His hazel eyes and light-brown hair shimmered in the window's reflected sunlight. "I was the only Basque kid in my class as a teenager. My accent, my history, my culture. They stood alone in the midst of a sea of Southerners. Cádiz is a long way from here."

"Flamenco and castanets come to mind."

Otxoa chuckled. "What do you think comes to mind when

Southerners talk about Euskadi?"

Death and destruction. But I didn't need to say it. "Must have been difficult."

"History is history. It is what it is. But I just got so tired of hearing about it. I lived in embarrassment of who I was and where I came from. Because of people like Xabi."

"Is that why your family relocated to the south?"

He nodded. "It was as far away from here as we could go without leaving the peninsula."

I took a moment to absorb this information. Otxoa and I had been companions for a substantial amount of time, so I knew a good amount of his past. Lots of stories from his time living down south. But his Basque stoicism hadn't been burned away in the Andalusian heat, so the more painful parts were rarely talked about. "So when you were assigned here . . ."

He shook his head. "I had a feeling it would happen. I'm Basque, I don't have any family up here, I speak Euskera. It was inevitable." He pursed his lips. "But I also knew I couldn't run from it forever. The choices we make, right?"

I turned to look out the window. As I gazed at the scenery, I wondered how many of these people felt the same mix of pride and shame that my companion felt. I had always figured, as an outsider looking in, that most Basques compartmentalized those coexisting, complex feelings— assuming those feelings coexisted at all.

We arrived at our stop and walked the remaining distance to the meeting. I went through the motions of greeting the

Hermanas, as well as Elders Ortega and Ramos, before settling in. As Elder Ramos began the meeting, my brain switched to autopilot and I began to daydream . . .

Three Months Earlier:

The morning rush at the bakery had subsided, so Kemina decided to sit down and chat with us.

"*Ay*, Elders, I'm exhausted!"

"Business is good, huh?"

"Business is good, yes. But business is also very tiring. How about you two? How's business?"

I smirked. "We're hanging in there. You Basques are a hard-headed lot."

Kemina and Otxoa feigned offense. "Hard-headedness is what's allowed us to thrive all these years. Hard-headedness and hard work. Right, Otxoa?"

He nodded in agreement. "It's true—but that also makes us very loyal. Once we commit to something, we get it done."

Kemina chuckled. "I envy your enthusiasm, Otxoa. I remember feeling the same way."

"What do you mean?"

Kemina bit her bottom lip contemplatively and drew in a breath. Looking at her watch, she said, "Let's take a walk. It's time to close for *siesta*, anyway."

"Sure. It's actually nice outside."

"Don't get too confident. You know how quickly—"

"—the weather can change, yes, we know," I said, jokingly.

As we walked down the street toward a small park, I could sense the gears inside Kemina's head were turning at full speed. "Elders," she said, "did you know I have a son?"

I was shocked. We'd known her all this time and hadn't known such an important detail about her. "No, we didn't. How come you haven't mentioned him before?"

"I'm a fairly private person. Hasn't always been that way. However, I've come to realize it's the life I prefer."

"How was your life before?"

She continued walking before answering. "My life before . . . was very different. I was young, headstrong, enthusiastic. I believed very passionately, like you do."

"Believed . . . in God?"

She smiled but quickly became serious. "No, nothing like that. Not for a long time. We stopped going to mass shortly after my First Communion, shortly after Franco died. I've returned a few times since, on Christmas or Easter, but . . . I don't think I'd be a welcome guest in God's house."

I felt sympathy for her. "I don't believe in a Father who doesn't want to hear from His children. As a mother, I'm sure you can relate. No matter what your son did, you'd never want him to feel as though he couldn't come to you for help."

Kemina looked at me before returning her gaze to an unknown object in the distance. "You're very good at this, Elder. But you're young, with young eyes and a young soul." We arrived at the park and sat down on a bench. "I remember what it was like to be young. That confidence, that surety, that . . . hard-headedness. It can drive away the ones you love the most. For better or worse, Elders, a time will come when you'll have to make a choice about whether or not your convictions and passions will dictate the course by which you imagined your life to go. And you can't expect them to converge. Life's just not that convenient."

"Why did you have to choose?" asked Otxoa.

"Because the life I was living and the life I wanted to live were mutually exclusive."

Otxoa and I continued to keep our gazes forward, reflecting on her words. My thoughts wandered to life before the mission and whether or not it would be an appropriate topic of conversation. I could offer to share with her what I'd learned during my time in Spain, hoping to make up for my own inexperience and find some common ground in conversations about individuals I'd known and experiences I'd had outside of Euskadi. However, as if able to communicate with each other telepathically, neither I nor Otxoa decided to divulge any details. We'd felt an impression to refrain from vainly trying to seem as if we were on her level in an attempt to impress, instead finding peace in choosing to believe the camaraderie we sought would be found in the silence.

In a more cheerful tone, Kemina continued, "If we're lucky enough, we'll all find something about which to be passionate in this life. And, if we're extraordinarily lucky, we'll find it when we're young, and it'll be worth doing." She took a deep breath and let it out. "Well, I think I'll head home to get some rest. Thanks for indulging me."

The three of us stood up. Kemina shot us a half-smile, and before parting, she said, "I'm not worried about you two, though."

I decided to indulge her a bit more. "Why's that?"

"Because you're young, with young eyes and a young soul. Because, like my son, you can't hide the passion you've already found while you're young, or the fact that, most importantly, you have a good heart."

Present Day:

"Elder?"

I snapped out of it and looked at Elder Ortega, who was waiting for an answer to whatever question it was he had asked me. "Sorry?"

"Elder Otxoa says you two have been making a lot of progress. Are you teaching anyone new?"

I shot a glance Otxoa's way. He looked at me a bit worriedly. I cleared my throat and said, "Yes, umm, yeah, we've met this young woman, her name is Amaia. She's a friend of Leire, from church. Seems genuinely interested, asks great questions, and our discussions are meaningful."

I could see out of the corner of my eye that Otxoa was smirking. I thought it was a pretty good answer, myself. However, I could also see that Hermanas Maduro and Casillas were unconvinced and amused at our poor attempts to conceal our deception.

"Elders, any chance you'll need someone to accompany you to the next visit, you know, in case she's alone at home, requiring the presence of a third party?" Maduro's expression didn't change, her question obviously a stab at something else. Did they know we had invaded their area? How could they have known?

Otxoa took this one. "We've only met a few times, always outdoors for simplicity's sake, but if we need an extra hand and no one else was available, we'll definitely give you a call."

The Hermanas smiled and looked at each other briefly, as if they were mentally shoveling bull droppings over their shoulder. They continued smiling as Casillas responded, "Sure thing, Elders. Always happy to help."

After the end of the meeting, Otxoa and I attempted to gather our things without making eye contact with the Hermanas. If they knew we had been in their area, it would be nearly impossible to deny.

We got up to head out and figured we'd grab a doner kebab for lunch. Just as we thought we were in the clear, I felt a tap on my back and heard that unmistakable Andalusian accent. I turned around to see Maduro looking like she had something on her mind. I looked over at Casillas, who was on a phone call. Otxoa had already made his way down the street.

"You've got a real knack for it," she said, nodding and smiling sarcastically.

I feigned ignorance. "What?"

"Storytelling. I've got to hand it to you. It was almost convincing."

Did she know? "Not sure what you're getting at."

Maduro seemed exasperated at my attempts to play dumb. "*Mira*, Elder, after a year of serving in the same cities and areas, I think we know each other pretty well. I'd like to think I know you well enough to know when something's off. Barakaldo is pretty far from your area. I mean, your friend's building is a block away from Iker Aranguren's Café. He knows it's our area and mentioned to us at church last Sunday a customer had seen two men in white shirts and ties getting out of a cab and entering a building in a dubious neighborhood. He thought it was strange that you'd be so far out of your area but figured maybe you were there to back us up. I've never known you or Otxoa to be this cagey. What's going on? You can tell me."

She was right. I could trust her. But I had orders from Capitana Martinez that this operation was to be conducted on a need-to-know basis. I lowered my voice before continuing. "I . . . know. I know I can. But I also can't. Do you understand?"

She furrowed her brow in confusion. "No, I don't. Does this have anything to do with your visit with Presidente?"

I shrugged. "I can't say."

She looked back at her companion, who was still on the phone, before continuing. "My gut tells me this has something to do with what happened to you guys. If I'm right, say nothing."

I continued to look her in the eye, my head slightly cocked to the side, my face expressionless.

Maduro cracked a smile. "You know my gut's never wrong."

She wouldn't budge. I glanced over at Otxoa, who glared at me impatiently from down the street while tapping his wrist. "Let's say your gut continued its winning streak," I said. "What would you want?"

Maduro looked relieved to finally be getting somewhere. "Casillas and I want in. I can't imagine going through what you and Otxoa went through. What they did, they did to all of us. And you can't just enter the lion's den without backup. You of all people should know that."

I was skirting the line too closely now. "Lion's den or not, we're not worried about it. Besides, Daniel ended up just fine."

Maduro, looking resigned, peered over my shoulder at Otxoa, then returned her attention to me and sighed. "I hope so, Elder. I hope you both know what you're doing."

CHAPTER 7

On the way back to the *piso*, we stopped as we passed a park that was currently less a bastion of fun for families and more a scene of impending chaos. At least a hundred people were assembled, yelling and chanting. They seemed to be directing their anger toward something obscured by trees.

"What did we stumble onto?" asked Otxoa.

I remained silent, shaking my head as I stared at the mass of angry people. I could feel my anxiety rising and began to question why we always had to be in the wrong place at the wrong time.

Suddenly, we were deafened by the sounds of sirens and engines bearing down on the park at full speed. We turned around to see two vans barreling down the street, one after the other. Both vans stopped about 30 yards in front of us, angled toward the park on the left-hand side of the street. The back doors of each van burst open, revealing at least a half-dozen armor-clad police officers looking ready for action. Each one donned a helmet and riot shield. A few of them also carried rifles. Emblazoned on the back of their Kevlar vests was the word *Ertzaintza*.

The paralysis was instantaneous. Time stood still. I was transfixed by the situation, memories flooding my conscience. The sirens, the uniforms, the commotion, the chaos . . . my senses kicked into high gear.

I saw the Basque Police enter the park.

I saw the mass of protestors begin to pull back, realizing a new threat had just arrived.

I heard the commander of the Ertzainas yell an order, causing the rest to fall into formation.

I saw each Ertzaina clutch a shield and press forward toward the protestors.

I saw two of the Ertzainas brandish their rifles and fire a volley of less-than-lethal warning shots in the protestors' general direction.

I felt this was the only warning the protestors would get.

I saw this didn't stop the angry mass from defying the invaders.

I saw and heard a dozen or so of them rush toward the line of Ertzainas in order to hurl insults. "*Zipaios!*" I heard them shout.

I saw the officers with the rifles fire rubber bullets into the crowd to subdue the more brazen of the demonstrators.

I saw a few of them fall, writhing in pain.

I saw that this seemed to be enough to disburse the majority of the group.

I felt the protestors' fear as they retreated.

Unable to move but fully aware of the danger of remaining where I stood, I managed to utter my companion's name.

Upon hearing this, Otxoa placed himself directly in front of me. He looked me in the eye and began to ask questions specifically aimed at shaking me out of it.

"Elder, what do you see?"

Using every ounce of mental fortitude I possessed, I answered him. "I see . . . I see you. I see trees. Grass. Light. Road. People."

"Good. What do you hear?"

Looking around and breathing heavily, I said, "Yelling. Broken glass. Rifles."

"What do you smell?"

"Engine exhaust. Burned rubber. Smoke."

"Good. Now, what do you feel?"

I began to calm down, steadying my breathing and taking stock of the situation. "A rush. I feel the adrenaline leaving my system. I'm okay . . . I'm okay."

Otxoa looked at me for a moment and said, "I thought those were supposed to subside."

Closing my eyes tightly before opening them again, I took a deep breath to compose myself. "Less intense is what the doctor said. They'll probably never subside."

Otxoa nodded. "You need a minute?"

I shook my head. "No, I'm good. Let's go."

CHAPTER 8

"So, you do this all day, every day, for two years?".

Otxoa nodded. "We do have one day each week, our preparation day, for laundry, grocery shopping, writing our families and friends, playing sports, or hitting the local tourist sites."

Xabi cocked his head to the side and narrowed his eyes. "What about girls?"

Otxoa chuckled. "For two years, we abstain from many things. Girls included."

He leaned forward, more interested. "No girls? For two years? *Madre mía* . . . but what about when you get home? You don't stay celibate your whole lives, right?"

"No, when we get home we can go out with girls, get married, start a family. You know, continue living life. These two years are sort of an intermission between the first and second acts of our lives."

"And the female missionaries, it's the same for them?"

"Yep. We live by the same rules."

Xabi sat back and shook his head. "I have to give it to you,

you've got stamina. Two years is a long time. Do you ever get homesick or miss your lives as regular dudes?"

Otxoa offered a slight shrug. "Yeah, sometimes. But these two years have been the best of my life."

Xabi looked at me. "And you? Best two years of your life too?"

"You have something for us?"

The way he looked at me told me he knew I had purposely avoided the question, but he decided to let it go. "Yeah, here. It's got some general information about the cell, along with a few very choice pieces of intelligence I've gleaned." He handed me a thumb drive, which I placed in my front pocket for the time being. "How do you plan on passing that along to Capitana Martinez?"

"I think it's best we keep that part a secret. Is this going to give Amalur to the feds?"

"What, you don't trust me?" said Xabi, facetiously, this time playing the part of the one ignoring the question. "I'm kidding. Hey, you're getting the hang of this."

"We're flattered." It was a stalemate.

Xabi smiled as he stood up and looked toward the boxes in the corner. "I've thought a great deal about what you talked about last time, you know, the choices we've made. I realized we've got more in common than I initially thought."

He seemed hesitant to continue, pacing back and forth a few times. The familiar pitter-patter of rain reached our ears as it caressed the windows.

"When I was a kid," Xabi said, "we were very poor. We didn't have much, but my mom refused to let me know. One year, for my birthday, my grandfather gave me a gold coin that he said had been found in a treasure chest on the deck of a Spanish galleon that sank off the coast of Africa hundreds of years ago. Whether or not that was the case, I never knew, but I thought it was the most amazing thing I would ever hold in my hands. I kept it in perfect condition, wrapped in a cloth and locked away in a box in my room.

"One day, I was invited to the birthday party of a kid in my class. I was excited because I never got invited to things like that. I was so happy. I ran home and told my mom. It was then, however, that I realized I had nothing to give him. I told her I didn't understand why we couldn't buy him a nice gift like the other kids.

"She said, '*Hijo*, what would make your heart happy?' Deep down, I knew what she meant, but I was so angry. I didn't want to give it up. So, for two days I fought against it, weighing if I should go to the party or stay home.

"When the day came, my mom asked me what I planned to do. I just cried and cried, not wanting to stay home but also not wanting to give up my treasure. 'I think you know what you're going to do,' she told me, 'because I know what I would do. And I know your heart.' I asked her how she could know, and she said, 'Because we share the same heart.' I finally understood my mom and how she was able to give so much of herself for me. She taught me what love really meant."

Holding back tears, I asked, "How did you feel? Sad? Empty?"

Xabi shook his head. "No, Elder, no. I felt like I was on top of the world. Like nothing could make me happier."

"You gave away your treasure."

Xabi nodded. "After I got home from the party, my mother had a present waiting for me. She told me she thought I deserved it, that I was ready."

Otxoa looked intrigued. "What did she give you?"

It was then that I noticed something I hadn't before. A glimmer of light originating from where Xabi was sitting, magnified by the occasional bouts of sunlight that pierced the clouds and poured through the window. He reached down and held the pendant of St. Ignacio, previously relegated to an oft-forgotten box, now displayed with pride around his neck.

I shook my head. "Why are you telling us this?"

Holding the pendant, he said, "Because it's only just recently that I've come to understand what this really means."

"What's that?"

Looking down at the pendant in the palm of his hand, he said, "That this wasn't simply my father's pendant. That my mother loved my father and wouldn't have saved this for me had he been the type of person to leave knowing he had a child on the way." He half-smiled. "That it wasn't the only thing by which she had to remember him. That this pendant, and not that gold coin, is the most amazing thing I've ever held in my hands."

CHAPTER 9

I'd heard so much about it that I had to come see it for myself on our preparation day. Or rather, the closest representation of the real thing available within the boundaries of the mission. "Wow . . . I don't even know where to start."

Hermana Maduro smiled as she nodded. "You should see the real thing in Madrid. It's incredible."

The streets were quiet in Guernica, making it easier to contemplate the mural of one of Pablo Picasso's most famous works of art. As I considered the history of this small town, the silence began to take on an eeriness. Fascist forces, at the request of General Franco, had obliterated this town and killed hundreds if not thousands of civilians in the process. This was done to quash rebellion in the north during Spain's brutal civil war, but it also served Hitler and Mussolini as they practiced their tactics and tested munitions for the global conflict that was already in its preliminary stages. Picasso painted this cubist masterpiece, aptly titled "Guernica," to express his anger and sadness at the death and destruction that his country had come to represent.

Hermana Casillas commented, "How tragic. As we were walking through the streets, I tried to picture what this place would have looked like after the bombing. Being here is . . . I don't know, kind of chilling." She squinted her eyes as she studied the work of art, as if trying to gain a deeper understanding of Picasso's inspiration. "I wonder if this place will ever be rid of the ghosts."

"The way things are going, Euskadi just seems like home for them." Taking a few steps toward the mural and crossing my arms, I considered the operation in which Otxoa and I were involved and if we would be able to help bring some relief to this part of the country that we loved so much, even if just for one person.

Out of the corner of my eye, I saw Otxoa start to show some of the photos on his camera to Casillas. They began chatting, so Maduro must have seen an opportunity to get an update from me. "So, how's your story?"

I turned my head slightly to look at her before turning back toward the mural. "It's . . . still being written." I looked down for a moment before looking at her. "It's not what I'd planned on doing during my final transfer. But we were all originally told that our assignment may be modified according to the needs of the mission president."

She stayed silent for a moment. "It's gotta be *some* modification."

I nodded, looking down again. "We're just . . . serving. Isn't that what we came to do? I feel alive again. I see clearly again. What Otxoa and I are doing gives us purpose."

"I get that." She took a deep breath and let it out. "My

brother was in the army. Did you know that?"

I shook my head. "I didn't. What's he doing now?"

"I don't know."

I looked at her, surprised by her answer.

She nodded. "He joined right after the 11-M bombings in 2004. Ended up in Afghanistan."

"How did your parents feel about that?"

Although she wasn't looking at me, I could sense she was delving into painful emotional territory; her eyes became slightly misty, and her shoulders were slumped. "Proud." She crossed her arms and looked over at me before looking forward again. "Very proud."

"How did *you* feel about that?"

She licked her lips as if to begin speaking but instead bit her bottom lip. "Scared. But also proud." She flashed me a brief smile. "I wished I could go with him, to protect him. Three months after he deployed, we received notice that he was missing. It tore my family apart. My parents blamed themselves."

My heart ached for her. "I'm so sorry. You never heard anything else?"

Maduro wiped away a single tear before clearing her throat and composing herself. "No, nothing. We were told to assume he was dead. My mother was nearly catatonic."

"Do you think he's alive?"

An entire minute seemed to pass in the few seconds that preceded her response. "No. I don't."

"Well, I hope your gut's wrong about that."

"It's never wrong, Elder."

Shaking my head, I said, "I know what you're doing."

"You're chasing the same dragon my brother went looking for in the desert."

I looked at her. "I've made my decision. *We've* made our decision. We've been given an opportunity. I know it sounds . . . corny, but I really believe this is what we were meant to do. There's something familiar, something special about this person. Something I can't quite place. Otxoa feels the same way. And maybe while we try to save some Basque souls, we can save a few Basque lives."

She stifled a smile forming at the corner of her mouth, then turned to face me. "Service. Opportunity. Adventure. Feeling alive. I've heard all that before. I know you think I'm being *pesada*. And maybe I am. But I've come to love these people too. I've come to understand what makes this place so wonderful. It's not at all what I had spent my whole life thinking it was. These are *real* Basque lives, whom I love. *Real* mothers and fathers, daughters and sons, sisters, and brothers. Come on, Elder, you have to know you can trust me. Let us help. We know what they're capable of doing. This is our country too, you know."

The remnants of our conversation quickly dissipated into the ether, to which only the ghosts of Guernica were now privy. I didn't have it in me to continue, and I sensed she was also running on fumes, emotionally. I shut my eyes and took a deep breath, trying to gain control.

"How do you deal with it?" I asked.

Sensing my distress, she reached over and gave my hand a squeeze. "I know there'll always be someone else to protect."

We came to an understanding, I think, in that moment, which took the form of a somber silence hanging in the air. It was as tangible a void of noise as had ever existed, but it said more than words could ever express.

Opening my eyes and sensing it was time to move on, I said, "1937 was a long time ago, right?" I pointed to the section of the mural showing a woman grieving over a dead body. "All I see is the present."

CHAPTER 10

"She hasn't made contact. Why hasn't she made contact?" Elder Otxoa sat nervously at the kitchen table, the cell phone within reach.

"Don't worry," I responded, "she will. The pamphlet was gone when we checked. Who else would have taken it?"

Over the last six weeks, our contact with Capitana Martinez had become less and less frequent, which meant she had learned to trust us with the integrity of the operation. Our dead drops seemed to be working as planned, and we understood the policy of "no news is good news" to be in effect. However, we were growing restless, desperate to know how the operation was progressing, especially since less than one week remained before the end of the transfer.

Otxoa picked up a piece of paper on the table. "Dude, I'm stressed. I can't stop looking at the date on this. Where did you put your trunky papers?"

"I don't know. That date has been burned into my mind. The last thing I need to do is to keep staring at the itinerary for my trip home."

"What happens if we're burned? Do you think Xabi will end up in prison?"

"I don't know. I wish there were some way to help, but I don't think there's anything we can do. Especially when Martinez keeps us in the dark."

Leaving the room, I realized that the truth of those words hadn't really sunk in until now. And, as Hermana Maduro had pointed out, these were real lives, and we were playing with live ammunition. We were essentially powerless to do anything other than continue to hold up our part of the bargain.

I walked over to the window to find some source of distraction on the street below. However, I knew the street wasn't an especially bustling one, and at 14:00 it was virtually abandoned.

I opened the window and rested my elbows on the warm windowsill. Feeling a cool breeze caress my face, I closed my eyes and attempted to shut out the fears, anxieties, and uncertainties that had staged a coup d'état in my mind and my soul and remained entrenched and unopposed for so long.

After about a minute, I opened my eyes and surveyed the lack of goings-on below. A man on a bicycle rounded the corner and rode down our street. I saw him stop in front of a building across from ours and ring the *timbre*. A brief conversation ensued before he walked back to his bicycle and got on. After a minute, a woman exited the building with a bike in tow. The two of them hugged, exchanged inaudible pleasantries, and rode off together.

Eureka.

I turned around to head to the kitchen. As soon as I walked

in, Otxoa could tell I was scheming. "Oh, no. What now?"

"What if there *were* something we could do?"

"You mean, like, get Xabi out?"

I nodded. "We'll contact Martinez and set up a meet. I'll bet if we put on enough of a show, we'll get the information we need."

Otxoa considered this for a moment before slowly nodding. "I can do that. What's the plan?"

"I don't know yet. But we have time to formulate something."

"He's been out of the country fairly recently. Maybe he could just return to where he was?"

I nodded slowly while drawing up plans in my head. "We'll have to keep this a secret. But I think this will be more than a two-man job."

My companion nodded, knowing exactly what I meant. "I'll call them. I know they've been dying to get in on this."

We were prematurely jolted out of our brainstorming session by the sound of the unique ringtone we had assigned to Capitana Martinez. Otxoa stood up, grabbed the phone, and threw it to me. He then walked over to the map of Bilbao on our living room wall. Hands on his hips, and with a newfound determination, he boldly declared, "It's a good thing we've got preparation day tomorrow. It's going to be a long night."

CHAPTER 11

The stream of *palabrotas* rushing out of Otxoa's mouth had practically no effect on Martinez. She seemed calm, but it was obvious she hadn't expected my companion to be so proficiently profane.

"I see the *chapa* you wear every day, but that is noticeably absent in this moment, doesn't completely override your Basque predilection to make such language a principle part of your vocabulary. I'll reiterate that I don't answer to you. And as far as our friend is concerned, don't get attached. If you knew what he'd done, you wouldn't hold him in such high esteem." She walked around the desk to where we were standing. "Look, I'm not completely unsympathetic to your situation. The intelligence we've received has been invaluable."

Taking on a compassionate tone now, she continued. "And I know that people can change . . . but I have to look out for the best interest of my people. And we can't take a risk with a wild card like Xabi."

Otxoa, although relaxed, was still up for a fight. "The

bridge you're burning is irreparable. If you do this, don't ever count on any further help. *Lehenean barka, bigarrenean urka* (the first time, forgive; the second time, hang)."

Martinez looked away for a moment, looking torn regarding the decision. Her gaze again met our eyes; first Otxoa's, then mine. Pausing a moment, she turned to lock the door and lowered her voice. "After I finish speaking, you will forget that this conversation ever happened. *¿De acuerdo?*"

We nodded.

"We're confident the information Xabi has provided is enough to wrap up this operation," she said. "We've got confirmation that Heriotza will soon be local, so we've decided to move on them. Sunday. 06:00."

So that was it. "Can we say goodbye?" I asked.

Martinez looked at me skeptically. "I suppose that would be fine. Keep it short. And keep your mouths shut."

As Otxoa and I turned to leave, Martinez stopped us. "I know this wasn't what you thought you'd be doing here, and I know you've been through a lot. But for what you've done, you have my thanks." Martinez eyed Otxoa and walked up to him, hand extended. "*Aldi luzeak, guztia ahaztu* (with time, all things are forgotten)."

Keeping a neutral expression, Otxoa looked at Martinez's hand. He looked back at her and, without breaking eye contact, made a show of removing his name tag from his pocket and clipping it to his shirt before begrudgingly shaking her hand. "*Arrotz-herri, otso-herri* (a foreign land is a land of wolves). Right, Capitana?"

Martinez eyed Otxoa's name tag and smiled wryly before nodding in agreement.

"Sunday, then," I said.

Martinez opened the door for us. "Elders, I have no idea what you're talking about."

The sun had set on our final Saturday in the city. As we ascended to Xabi's floor, I couldn't help but feel as though we should clue him in on both Martinez's plan and ours. "We're taking an awful risk by keeping our word to Martinez."

Otxoa sighed. "I know. But it's a risk either way. We don't want to make promises we can't keep."

We walked into the *piso* to find Xabi sitting on the floor in the corner, looking at photos. A bottle of *something* was sitting next to him, and it looked like he'd been through half of it. "Elders, come in."

"What do you have there?" I asked. He handed me a stack of photos, and I began to flip through them.

Xabi smiled and poured himself another glass, looking at it before taking a drink. "*Sagardoa* . . . cider. Without a doubt, nectar of the gods."

Otxoa and I sat down and continued studying the photos. Some of them were of Xabi as a child, playing soccer, swimming, spending time with his grandparents. Others looked more recent. One of the photos Otxoa was holding caught my attention. "When was this taken?"

Xabi looked at the photos. "About six months ago. I had hit all the touristy spots, so I went for a drive in the countryside. There was a lake about an hour outside of town. Once I got there, I rented a boat and took it out to the middle." He got up and walked over to Otxoa, taking the photo from his hand. "I'd never felt more peace in my entire life. Despite the things in which I had been involved, despite the people with whom I was involved, despite being away from everything and everyone I knew . . . the sun was shining, the water was still and clear, and it was like I was the only person in the world."

"Sounds incredible. Sounds like heaven."

"It was, almost. It felt like a dream, like something surreal. That's how I'd like to go out, I think. In fact, I hadn't felt that way since I gave away that coin. And I haven't felt it since . . ." He looked over at us. ". . . until about six weeks ago."

The guilt began to weigh heavier now. I held critical information that I promised to guard, but that could save his life if I disclosed it. I didn't know what to do.

Xabi studied the photo for a moment longer before replacing it in the box. He refilled his glass and closed the bottle. "It's harder to believe in people than it is to believe in God. To do what you do, you have to believe. You *really* have to believe in people."

"Everyone has that choice," I said. "Including you."

He downed the rest of his glass. "Do you really believe that?"

I nodded.

Xabi looked at Otxoa. "And you?"

"We Basques have to be loyal to one another. We want the same thing. That's a choice I had to make before we even met."

Xabi looked at him, then at the painting of the man and the boy on a boat. "I hope that's the truth. And I hope one day I can get there. Who knows? You know how quickly the weather can change."

My heart sank. It must have been all over my face, too, and all over Otxoa's, because Xabi could sense the change in our demeanor. I finally realized why he seemed so familiar. I couldn't believe we hadn't put the pieces together.

"What did you say?" I asked.

"I said, you know how quickly the weather can change. Wouldn't want to get caught in the rain . . ."

Ten Weeks Earlier:

Thumbing through Kemina's photo album, Otxoa pointed to a photo that caught his attention. "Is this . . . ?"

"My son, yes. Ander." Kemina picked up the photo and looked at it fondly. "He's got his grandfather's black hair and full, bushy beard." She passed the photo my way.

"Where is he now?"

"He's studying in France. He'd never say so, but I think he believes that's where his father is."

"Is it?"

Kemina smiled. "I don't know. And that's the truth. I got pregnant, but he left before Ander was born."

"Did he know you were pregnant?"

Kemina shook her head.

"Did you try to tell him?"

She held out her hand, and I returned the photo. "It wasn't his fault. I made choices that can't be undone. I've made my peace with that. That's all I can do. That's all any of us can do."

"How much does Ander know?"

"He knows enough. He's passionate too, you know. He gets that from me."

Otxoa finally asked the question that had lingered for some time. "What were you so passionate about?"

Kemina took a deep breath and looked as if she were mentally traveling back in time. Sunlight shone through the window, providing us with a welcome measure of warmth. "I think I was passionate about the *idea* of being passionate. And there were those who took advantage of that. Even the devil can cite scripture to suit his purpose."

"But things changed."

She nodded as she looked longingly at the photo. "A second chance."

"Baking?"

She laughed. "It was my parents' bakery and my grandparents' before them. I grew up around it. We never had much in the way of money, but we always had enough to eat. If you have bread, you have life. I remembered how much of a community staple it was. Fresh warm bread and pastries. They represented hope and goodness. But man does not live by bread alone, right? I guess I've always associated this place with life, so I decided to take it a step further and make it a haven for those looking for that same second chance."

I nodded, understanding. "In other words, a way to get back into His good graces."

"*Exacto*. And if not into *His* good graces, at least into my own. To allow me to sleep at night, provide for my son, my real second chance, and show him that to do good is a choice. Right, Otxoa?"

Otxoa smiled. "I think you and my mom would be friends."

"I'd like that. She's welcome here anytime."

Present Day:

This was it. The cards were on the table. His face now resembled ours. He knew that we knew. He and I stared at each other for a moment that seemed to last an eternity. A high-pitch noise filled my head and I felt blind, deaf, and dumb.

I broke the silence. "Ander."

He continued to look me in the eye, but his face looked tense and he seemed to be in fight-or-flight mode. "She told you. Martinez told you, didn't she?"

"She didn't tell us anything."

He stood up, looking shaky. "But . . . you knew her."

I nodded while trying to reconcile my emotions. Martinez hadn't told us. Not one thing.

He walked over to the dresser on the other side of the room. "So that's why she chose you. Martinez had to have known that you knew my mom. Had to have known you were trustworthy and capable. My mom would have vouched for you."

Otxoa and I, while still trying to keep our feet on solid ground after the bombshell that had been dropped on us, now had another mystery to uncover. But that would have to wait, because my incorrigible Basque companion spoke up first.

"Yeah, you're damn right she would have vouched for us. You think Martinez just drove by one day and asked us if we wanted to play the messenger? You think we're what's been lacking in this decades-long fight?"

Ander clenched his jaw and looked Otxoa square in the eye. "Then what the hell *are* you doing here?"

Sensing the coming storm, I stepped in. "How did Martinez know your mother?"

Ander looked at himself in the mirror over the dresser before using the reflection to look at us. "She used to be, you know, like me. The apple doesn't fall very far, eh? After I was born, she decided to steer her life in another direction. We had to leave the country for a time while things died down. It's not easy to get out. And it's even more dangerous to return. You can ask Otxoa about what happened to Yoyes."

"When did you learn your mom was working with the government?"

"Not until I reached out after returning to Bilbao. In fact, it was only then that I learned the whole story."

"That she was an informant?"

Ander shook his head. "No. That was just a byproduct of what she was really doing."

"What was she doing? Trying to plant informants within the organization?"

Ander turned around to face us and crossed his arms. Again, shaking his head, he said, "She wasn't getting people *in*. She was getting them *out*."

A haven, she had called it. A flood of memories washed over me. My emotions again began to remind me who was boss, barreling down on me like a freight train. I clenched my fists to help get myself under control. "You came back and took her place."

Ander looked away. His arms were still crossed as he leaned against the dresser, facing us. He rocked back and forth for a moment. "We'd been trying to discover the source of our leak for some time. The Ertzaintza and the Guardia Civil had been one step ahead of us for a couple of years. At first, we thought they were either lucky or just astute. It wasn't until about six months ago that we discovered there had to be a mole within the cell. Immediately, we set out to find it. About two months ago, I was told we had a lead. We learned that not only was this person leaking information, but they were working with someone on the outside who was facilitating the extraction of vulnerable individuals from the organization."

"Kemina. But you didn't know, at that time, she was the one on the outside."

He shook his head. "We had to act fast. We determined who the most likely candidates were to be turned and gave each of them a separate piece of seemingly important, but ultimately false, intelligence." Ander walked back over to the other side of the room to grab a drink. "We waited for the mole to funnel the information to the authorities. When it was incvitably acted on, we would know who the mole was."

"What did you do?"

"Nothing. At that point, only the leadership was privy to the details of the plan. I was told not to worry about it."

"Did you think anything of that? Was it unusual?"

"I wasn't sure. I hadn't been in long and didn't think I had the seniority for things like this. But I also couldn't shake the feeling that the information had been specifically withheld from me."

"Is that when you decided to come back?"

Ander was silent. His expression was neutral, and he looked down at the ground. The longer he remained silent, the worse I felt. The feeling in the pit of my stomach grew more intense, and there was nothing I could do to stop it. And what's worse, I felt like what he hesitated to say to us would only make the feeling more powerful.

"No," he said softly. "The plan was in motion, and I didn't even know where it would happen." He returned to his seat and slumped down.

"When did you find out?"

"The same day it happened. Between the news and the whisperings amongst the rest of the organization, I pieced it together." Ander looked as if he were watching this movie play out on some projector, unseen by anyone but him. He looked down into his glass. "Everyone started congratulating me. I didn't understand why."

I could feel Otxoa's demeanor shift without even looking in his direction. Ander seemed to feel the same way, and his posture turned slightly defensive. I was the slowest in the room, since it took those two things to make me realize what this meant.

"You," I said, my mouth agape in bewilderment.

Ander didn't acknowledge my accusation. He looked away before saying, softly, "Every bombmaker has a signature . . ."

Otxoa exploded. "You *killed* her! *You* killed her!"

I immediately got up from my seat to put myself between the two of them. Otxoa was often quick to react, but he had never let his emotions cause him to get physical, even in the worst of times.

"*She* was the future! *She* was the good!" he said, barely controlling himself. Taking a few breaths and calming down, he said, "She was Euskadi." He began to undo the buttons on his right sleeve. "You asked why we're here. You want to know why?"

Otxoa rolled up his sleeve to reveal a scar measuring about twenty centimeters in length, running from his wrist to the inside of his elbow. Ander's eyes went wide in disbelief. Otxoa nodded without breaking eye contact.

"Wrong place, wrong time. Collateral damage. Go ahead, take a good look. I've got your signature on my arm as a *recuerdo.*"

He continued to display his scar before shooting an upward nod in my direction. I lifted my shirt to expose a jagged, fifteen-centimeter X-shaped scar on my left side.

"They tell me the smell of garlic, the one that will linger with us forever, comes from the white phosphorus you added." Otxoa rolled up his sleeve. "We're here because *you* fired the first shot. *We* saw a chance to fire the last."

They squared off in Euskera. I couldn't understand a word they were saying, but from their body language I gathered their emotions were turning from anger to sadness, and from sadness to despair. I did, however, catch the word "*ama,*" or "mother."

Otxoa began to repeat a phrase in Basque. He quickly glanced over at me before switching to Castellano. "Say it! I want you to say it! I want to hear it!"

Ander stood up, fighting back tears. "She was my *mother!*"

After letting the silence reign for a few moments, I felt it was my turn to speak up. I began, softly, "Ander, every experience is either the worst thing to happen or it's a chance to start anew. The scars you carry, the ones we carry, are all alike in that they'll affect us—albeit in different ways and to varying degrees—forever." I touched my scar. "Otxoa and I can cover these up. You could even go your whole life without talking about what happened, you know, talking about your scars. But it's your choice."

Ander composed himself before responding. "You never answered my question."

"What?"

"After everything . . . can you look me in the eye and tell me that these two years, *especially* the past two months, have been the best of your life?"

I paused to search the depths of my heart for the truth. Even before I knew what I was going to say, I started speaking. "When you asked me, I didn't answer because I didn't know. Before everything that happened, I thought I was really making a difference, really serving. I thought I was doing what I was meant to be doing. But these past few months have been a whirlwind of emotions for me. We deal with these things the best we can. We could choose to see ourselves as victims of unfortunate circumstances, choose to see what happened as the worst thing ever. And we'd be justified in doing so."

I continued, relying on what was in my heart but what my brain hadn't yet figured out. "But Otxoa and I, we choose to see ourselves as survivors. And while Otxoa is right, we didn't get involved thinking we were the only ones who could bring about change. We've chosen to see it as a way to fulfill our purpose, to justify our existence, and to prove that we *always* have a choice." I paused. "The best two years? No, but it's been one hell of an adventure."

Ander, in tears, looked at Otxoa and gestured to me. *"Puro Vasco?"*

Otxoa smiled and nodded. *"Puro Vasco."*

CHAPTER 12

I couldn't hear the sound of the rhythmic breathing signaling that Otxoa had fallen asleep, so I assumed the same anticipation that kept me awake at 02:00 kept him from sleeping too.

"*Oye*, Otxoa," I whispered.

"Yeah, I can't sleep either."

"You ever think about walking the Camino de Santiago?"

He didn't respond right away. "Of course. It crosses everyone's mind up here. What better way to prepare, right? Two years of walking and talking to people from all over the world. Every day, a continuation of the same adventure. A destination. A beginning and an end."

A beginning and an end.

"I'll bet at the beginning of your mission you never thought this is how it would end, huh?"

He laughed. "You know what I never thought would end? You remember when we went to eat with the Dias family in the *pueblo* . . ."

DAN STEVENS

Two Months Earlier:

Hermana Maduro's voice over the phone was frantic. "Elders? Where are you? The bus is leaving!"

There's a reason why cross-country athletes wear the bare-minimum amount of clothing necessary to compete. Oh, and also why they wear appropriate footwear. Nobody wants to sprint full speed in a suit jacket, slacks, and dress shoes.

We had cut it too close to catch the last bus out of the *pueblo* and into Bilbao. Having to stop by the ATM because the driver wouldn't take either a credit card or an empty *bono* card (bus pass) ate into precious minutes that would have been better served actually making it to the bus stop on time.

Otxoa looked at me frantically and said, "We're going to have to run."

I didn't even question the decision. We took off toward the stop, passing one unhelpful sign after the next, and I began to wonder if we were going the right direction. The sun beat down on the remains of the afternoon showers, causing the road beneath our feet to glow.

Spotting a trio of old-timers, we stopped our sprint and asked how far we'd have to go to reach the bus stop. They looked flabbergasted, and with good reason—two Mormon Missionaries were running full speed in suits and ties through their *pueblo*.

One gentleman extended his hand and said, "It's about five hundred yards that way. But I don't think you'll get there in time."

Refusing this dose of Basque pessimism, we continued our marathon across town, desperately hoping to find our destination. After a search that began to feel never-ending, we caught the scent, figuratively, and followed the signs pointing us in the right direction.

As we approached the bus stop, we spotted the promising omen of a passenger seated on the bench. "It hasn't arrived yet," I got out between labored breaths.

We slowed down and came to an abrupt halt, surprising the passenger. "*Kaixo* (hello)," said Otxoa. She nodded.

I sat down on the bench triumphantly, and the two of us started laughing. No matter how much we wiped it away with our sleeves, the sweat streaming down our faces just kept coming. I took off my coat and loosened my tie and shirt collar. Otxoa followed suit and began to fan himself with the daily planner in his shirt pocket.

Just then, the bus came around the corner and sped up toward our stop. I gathered my things, eager to ascend the steps to the air-conditioned palace that awaited.

I did notice, however, that the passenger who had also been waiting for the bus did not get up. I figured she was either just waiting until the last moment or, possibly, for another bus. To our absolute horror, the bus sped up and blew right past our stop. In the window, I could see Hermana Casillas waving to us, a look of soul-crushing pity on her face.

I looked at Otxoa, and we began our Olympic-worthy sprint yet again, fighting against the expired adrenaline that lingered in our veins. I wasn't sure how much longer I could last.

By some miracle, the bus came to a stop about fifty yards down the road. Once we arrived, we paid the fare and boarded. The passengers looked astonished, but we pressed on toward the back where Casillas and Maduro were waiting.

Casillas could hardly contain her laughter. "I asked the bus driver to please stop and let you guys on. You can thank me later."

"Alright, alright. Laugh. At this point, I just don't care."

Maduro pulled out her camera and snapped a photo of the two of us, which I was sure she'd mercilessly use while telling this story for weeks to come. "That's so I can prove I know two future world-famous Olympic athletes."

Thirty minutes later, with renewed strength after our cross-country sprint, we bid the Hermanas farewell and stepped off the bus and into the cool, crisp Bilbao air.

"I don't know about you, but I'm craving some dessert," I said. "The food was delicious, but I need a little something extra. You want to grab something on the way to our next appointment?"

Otxoa patted his stomach in agreement. "You read my mind."

We began our stroll toward Kemina's bakery. The sun began to set on what had been an eventful yet beautiful day. Conditions were perfect for a leisurely stroll to our favorite spot in the city. We'd be able to stop by and get to the next appointment with a few minutes to spare.

Otxoa let out an exaggerated breath. "Man, the Hermanas saved our freakin' lives. We should pick up something for them before the next district meeting."

"No kidding. We owe them, and *then* some."

We continued walking before stopping at a crosswalk to wait for the traffic to pass. Otxoa was staring off into the distance at a group of girls on the other side of the plaza.

"See your future girlfriend?"

Otxoa shot me a glance and smirked. "You jealous?"

"Whatever, man. You know I'll be back to give you some competition."

He laughed and shook his head. "*Puro Vasco*. When you come back, I'm going to show you around *my* town." He took another look at the group of girls. "Bilbao is beautiful, but San Sebastián is heaven."

I chuckled and repeated what he had said inquisitively. "*Puro Vasco?*"

"*Puro Vasco*. Accept it; this is your home now."

Present Day:

". . . Yeah, man, never again. *Never* again."

Otxoa continued laughing. It then turned into the type of belly laugh I hadn't heard from him in months. It was infectious. I began to laugh, and soon we were both on the floor, unable to breathe as we wiped the tears away.

He managed to get a few words out. "*Hombre*, we were recruited by the Guardia Civil's Interpol liaison to be the go-between in an intelligence-gathering operation involving an ETA bombmaker-turned-informant. How did we end up here?"

"I don't even know why I'm laughing! I'm so tired. I . . ."

"I know, it's late. What are we doing? We need to be in Barakaldo in, like, two hours."

Our laughing began to subside. "No, man, I mean, I'm *tired*. Mentally, physically, emotionally. . . I'm exhausted. "

Otxoa was silent for a moment. "Spiritually?"

"What?"

"You left out 'spiritually.' Seems like you left it out on purpose."

He was right. I had tried to do anything I could to avoid thinking about it. "You're not?"

He laughed again. "Yeah, man, of course I am. And of course you are. No shame in that. Not after all we've seen. Not after all we've done."

"You think we did everything we could?"

"No, but I think we'll have done everything we can in a few hours."

"I mean, as missionaries. As far as this operation is concerned, we've done all we know how to do and then some. But as missionaries, did we do everything we could?"

"You mean, did we serve him? Did we love him as our neighbor, even after what he did? If you can answer yes, then yeah, I think we did our job. And we laugh so that we don't cry, man."

Neither one of us said anything else before Otxoa drifted to sleep. I thought about that day in the *pueblo*, and how much I wished it had ended differently. I thought about Kemina, and whether or not she would have seen this as the culmination of her family's penance.

Finally, I felt tired enough to drift off to sleep. I looked over at the clock. It was almost time now.

Two Months Earlier (continued):

Being that we were in Euskadi, the clouds decided again to assert their dominance by giving us fifteen minutes of uninterrupted rain, even when I could have sworn they'd decided to give us the day off. After our impromptu track meet in the *pueblo*, it was most welcome.

We arrived at Kemina's about thirty minutes before closing. "Elders, great to see you!" she said, her warm smile serving as our welcome. "Come on in out of the rain and get warm. I've got a few *napolitanas* left."

"*Buenas*, Kemina," responded Otxoa. "That's the best news I've heard today."

"I wouldn't want your mother thinking we don't take care of you here. How is she?"

"She's fine. Down south, she's probably enjoying a warm evening and a cloudless sky."

She scoffed. "*Andalucía* . . . frequently cloudless skies? Not very Basque of you, Otxoa."

"I couldn't agree more," I said.

He grimaced and raised his eyebrows. "Some sun every now and then wouldn't be terrible. It keeps things balanced. Everything in moderation, right?"

She smiled and gestured for us to take a *napolitana*, her long, dark hair swinging back and forth as she walked behind the counter.

Covering my mouth as I chewed, I asked, "Have you heard from Ander?"

"He called me last month, but he prefers to communicate via WhatsApp. He hasn't sent me a message in a while, though. But you know how it is."

I nodded as I enjoyed a bite of my *napolitana*. Closing my eyes and taking a deep breath, I let the air out through my nose. *Buenísimo.*

Kemina checked her watch and looked surprised. "Elders, I need to step out for a moment to make a call. Watch the place for me, okay?"

We gave her the thumbs up, as our mouths were otherwise occupied.

"I do believe she holds my heart," I said, gazing longingly at my pastry. Otxoa nodded in agreement. He took the cell phone out of his pocket and checked the time. We had about fifteen minutes until our next visit, and it would take us ten to arrive from here. "We have to run right after she gets back. Hope she doesn't *tardar.*"

After a few minutes, she returned. She looked a bit *off*, as if she were on autopilot. It was almost like she forgot we were there.

"*Todo bien?*" pried Otxoa.

She snapped out of it. "Yes, all good." She focused her gaze our way for a moment before turning it toward something out on the street. "Elders, what will you do when you finish your mission?"

I looked at Otxoa and laughed. "He wants to start a business and become Euskadi's richest bachelor, or he wants to do some traveling. Or, he wants to find a nice girl and settle down. I don't know. It depends on the day."

Otxoa pretended to take offense by making the *ma che vuoi* hand gesture typical to Spaniards and Italians. "Not sure what my plans are yet, but I'll be back."

Just then, a group of young women walking by the bakery looked inside and smiled at Otxoa and me. Kemina squinted her eyes, smiled wryly, and began pointing at me. "Yeah, I bet you'll be back. You'd better be careful. If you come back, you might not ever lea—"

And before she could finish her sentence, I experienced a sensory overload as my reality came crashing down around me.

BOOM.

I found myself on my back, having trouble breathing without understanding why. My chest felt heavy, as if someone were sitting on it. I felt the full force of the shockwave that sent me flying backwards.

Adrenaline rushed through my veins, dulling the pain temporarily, but I knew it wouldn't last. From my head to my toes, I felt sensations I had never felt before, and although the adrenaline shielded me from the worst of it, my injuries would have run the gamut: aches, pains, cuts, bruises, and possibly breaks and burns.

Comprehending the magnitude of this was difficult since my eyes stung from the copious amount of debris in the air. There was so much of it that I could hardly make out my surroundings. I sat up, hoping to catch a glimpse of Otxoa or Kemina, but couldn't find either of them. The entire bakery was gutted and completely unrecognizable.

Despite the sheer pandemonium, I couldn't hear a thing. My ears were killing me, becoming inundated with a piercing sound unlike any I had ever experienced. I figured my eardrum must have burst.

Tasting blood, I slowly put my hand up to my mouth but discovered the blood was flowing from my nose. I blindly patted myself down to see if anything was missing, but the damage seemed manageable for now.

As I regained my other senses, I was hit with an

overwhelming scent of garlic. My first thought was that the blast had altered my sense of smell. The smell of garlic was soon joined by smoke, fire, burning rubber, and another that was worse than anything I'd ever smelled before.

I had to get up and out of the building since it could collapse at any minute. I wiped away the dirt, blood, and sweat from my face. I needed to keep the debris at bay, so I took off what was left of my tie and held it over my nose and mouth.

"Otxoa! Kemina!"

No response.

I slowly stood up, testing my legs to see if they were still functional. As I staggered to my feet and shuffled forward, I scoured the remnants of what was once a haven. Dozens of thoughts raced through my head as I slowly made my way around the hollowed-out bakery. I wondered where they were, if another blast would occur, and if I was unknowingly seriously injured. I imagined the building caving in or some sinister figure entering the wreckage of the blast to finish off the survivors.

I stopped and did everything I could to ward off the thoughts. Closing my eyes, I steeled myself to continue on. I opened them again and called out, "Kemina! Where are you? Otxoa!"

I overheard some muffled sounds to my right. Slowly heading toward the noises, I began to make out the shape of my companion, whose jacket had been shredded in the explosion. He had taken it off and bunched it up. Almost as if he were using it for . . .

Kemina. She was lying next to him, unconscious, one leg

caught under some concrete. Otxoa was using his jacket to apply pressure to an unseen wound. I made it over to where they were and looked for a way to help. That was when I noticed she wasn't the only one in need of assistance. Otxoa had a deep gash in his right arm, which needed immediate attention.

"Hurry, take my belt," he said and pointed to an area just above his elbow. "Wrap it here and pull tight."

I did as he instructed, and he winced as the pain surely became nearly more than he could bear. He continued applying pressure to Kemina's wound, which looked to consist of a nasty hole in her gut.

"What can I do?" I asked frantically.

Otxoa appeared exasperated and looked at me with uncharacteristically dark, panicked eyes. Both of us were in disbelief over what was happening, but we both understood that now wasn't the time to dwell on it.

He began to break down. "I don't . . . I don . . . I don't know." He began to desperately look around before shaking his head and shooting me an agonizing look. I looked down at an unconscious Kemina. The amount of blood pouring out of her stomach wound was more than I had ever seen at one time in real life. I looked at Otxoa, returning that same, agonizing look.

I positioned myself on the other side of her body in an effort to look for something, anything I could do to help. I knew, deep down, that this was the end for her, but at least I could try to give her some peace or comfort before she passed. Not finding any immediate opportunities to render aid, I closed my eyes and said a quick prayer.

Opening my eyes, I saw that Otxoa's head was inclined, and he had ceased applying pressure to her wound. Paralyzed with fear or disbelief, or both, he still held his now darkened jacket while he stared at her lifeless body. I looked down at her face and felt an immense sadness.

Forcing myself to shift gears, I turned my attention to my companion and his bleeding arm. "That looks bad. Let's get out of here."

I stood up and reached over to help him stand. At first he resisted, but then he relented and stood up. We leaned on each other as we walked out of Hell and into the street. My stomach sank as I surveyed the extent of the carnage. The death and destruction, it appeared, had not confined itself to Kemina's bakery; several other buildings were also badly damaged.

Remnants of cars, road, sidewalk, and other assorted debris covered the once peaceful city street. A white fog had spread from where we were standing to the end of the street, slowly dissipating as it rose into the darkening evening sky.

Otxoa pointed to nails that had been lodged into the sides of buildings, cars, and anything else unfortunate enough to have been caught in their path, including some bodies. Several of the bodies were strewn across the street in various states of disarray. Some were only slightly injured, while others were missing limbs, or worse.

We walked past an overturned vehicle and instantly regretted it as I identified the source of the terrible scent: the driver had been so badly burned that I wasn't even certain it was a person.

I looked at my companion. He was surveying the chaos

unfolding around us, and his face said it all. He looked at me with a gut-wrenching look in his eyes and said, "*Puro Vasco.*"

Emergency medical personnel began to arrive and assess the situation. They ran up to Otxoa and me, asking where we were hurt. One of the paramedics immediately got to work on Otxoa's arm.

I waved off the second paramedic, but she started speaking to me frantically, pointing to my left side, which sported a growing red stain. Her words became muffled and I began shaking my head, realizing that everything had happened so fast that my brain couldn't fully process the amount of pain I was supposed to be in until that moment.

I looked down to see a sharp piece of metal sticking out of my side and my extremities become shaking noodles as the adrenaline slowly left them.

Then I passed out.

CHAPTER 13

Abruptly, I awoke from the nightmare, sweating. I reached down to my side and felt the scar.

Otxoa was already dressed and ready to leave. "Hey, Elder, it's okay. Everything's fine. It's time to go."

I nodded and composed myself before quickly getting dressed and grabbing my bag, which was already ready to go. We knelt in front of the door and Otxoa said a prayer.

"*¿Listo?*"

"*Vamos.*"

We quietly exited the *piso* and headed downstairs. Before going out the front door, we looked outside to see if anyone was roaming the streets at 04:00. We didn't see anyone, so we proceeded to exit the building.

Upon conceiving our plan, we had realized that our biggest obstacle would be actually getting to Barakaldo. Walking was impractical. A cab or ridesharing service would create too much exposure, and we'd be logged in their database. Public transportation presented us with the same exposure problem, not to mention it wouldn't be available for another hour at least. And we definitely weren't going to be hotwiring anything.

We decided that, because it would still be dark outside, we'd be able to bike the distance in a reasonable amount of time while retaining the flexibility to make deviations, if necessary, and remain anonymous.

The Hermanas had bought bikes off of the street the day before, painted them black, and stowed them in our lobby overnight. Both of us were dressed in black from head to toe, with a spare change of clothes in our backpacks.

The goal was to get to Ander's *piso* without detection before the raid was to take place. I would hide in the alley next to the building and call a taxi. Otxoa would change into normal clothes, enter the building, and extract Ander. The taxi would take him to a location outside of the city where he'd be greeted by Hermanas Maduro and Casillas. Even we wouldn't know his final destination.

The riskiest part of the ride would begin when we got onto the N-634 highway, as that would be where we'd be most visible, not to mention it'd be the longest stretch of the trip. Instead of taking the exact route we were given by the GPS, we would stick to side streets until merging onto the highway was absolutely necessary.

Before leaving, I reviewed the GPS instructions and couldn't help but shake my head when reading the names of the streets, some nearly unpronounceable. Handing the GPS to Otxoa, I said, raising my eyebrows and grimacing, "I'll follow *you*." He chuckled, knowing exactly what I meant.

We got on our bikes and began the journey across the city. Although the GPS told us it would be a twenty-six-minute ride, we figured we'd need more time than that. Granted, no one would be privy to our plan; however, if, upon investigation of Ander's disappearance, someone mentioned to the Guardia Civil that they saw two young men riding bikes toward Barakaldo at 04:00, it wouldn't take Martinez long to figure out we were the culprits.

From our *piso* in Indautxu, we rode down Egaña Kalea toward Etxaniz Suhiltzailearen Plaza, where Egaña Kalea became Pérez Galdós Kalea. At the end of Pérez Galdós Kalea was Basurtuko Hospital. At this point, we could have headed toward the highway, but we decided to ride through the hospital's parking lot and then cut through side streets. Eventually, we dropped into Olabeaga Aldapa, which led us to the N-634.

The traffic was heavier than we had anticipated. So much so, in fact, that it became not so much a matter of remaining unseen as it did a matter of remaining inconspicuous.

Biking. On the highway. At 04:00. In all black.

Fortunately, the darkness of the early morning, combined with the velocity at which we traveled, would make it impossible for our faces to be identified.

I felt the lactic acid buildup in my legs and could only assume the same for Otxoa. I thought about Kemina and how hard she worked for the land she loved so much, even giving her own life to do so. She had taught us what real conviction looked like, and I wondered if I could ever be so convinced of a cause for which to give my life.

I thought of Ander and the grief and despair that he must be living with every day. I hoped Kemina would be proud of Ander and our efforts to get him out of this life, and, by doing so, staying true to her advice to find something that gave us true fulfillment.

Before I knew it, we were crossing the River Cadagua and exiting the N-634, flying down Zumalakarregi Kalea, which became Obispo Padre Olaetxea Plaza. Larrea Kalea and Reketa Kalea were the last two streets on which we traveled before starting our approach toward Barakaldo's city center.

The first leg of our plan was nearly complete.

Creeping toward the city center, we noticed more activity than was normal this early in the morning. Otxoa and I, breathing heavily, slowed down to plan out how we would arrive surreptitiously.

"Just a few more streets," he said, doubled over from exhaustion.

"Seems a bit busy, don't you think?"

Otxoa nodded and squinted as he tried to catch his breath. "We have to be careful. Come on."

We rode slowly along the streets, inching closer to the target location. In the distance, there was muffled yelling accompanied by a flickering light, accentuated by its stark contrast with the dark Basque sky.

A feeling of dread began to grow in the pit of my stomach. The closer we got, the more I worried about everything falling apart. We were so close now. We couldn't fail him. We could not fail *them*.

At one hundred yards from our destination, we stopped and rested the bikes against a wall. Finding a deserted alleyway with some cover, we changed into our nice, sweat-free clothes. We then made sure the coast was clear before continuing on foot toward the apartment building. The flickering light grew brighter as the voices grew louder and more intense.

At about fifty yards, we spotted what would be the first of several heavy-duty vehicles. Some had *Ertzaintza* emblazoned on the side; others *Guardia Civil*. This was not good. Did they know? How could they have known? Unless . . .

Martinez. She had lied to us. She had to have known we would try something. Which meant we had missed our chance. Everything we had planned, everything we had hoped for, everything we had wanted . . . was gone.

As we got closer to the scene, remaining mostly out of sight of any patrolling authorities, what we saw was jaw-dropping. The damage that had been done to Ander's building was incomprehensible. Why would this have happened? Could Heriotza have been here? A crowd of people gathered around the makeshift perimeter. Maybe we could get some information if we got close enough.

"This is all you," I said to Otxoa.

He nodded and approached one of the Ertzainas. In Euskera, he asked, "What the hell happened here?"

The Ertzaina eyed him warily but didn't seem to consider Otxoa a threat. "Stay back. We're still securing the area. There could be more explosives."

"Explosives?"

"You didn't hear it?"

"Uh, no, I'm . . . a heavy sleeper."

"It's an ETA safe house. One of the Guardias got overzealous and nearly blew us all to hell. No casualties, though. Well, at least on our side."

"Were any of the Etarras killed?"

The Ertzaina nodded. "A few, I believe. I didn't go in, but there was some gunfire. Didn't last long."

"So there was more than just the one?"

"Just the one?"

Otxoa must have realized his slip of the tongue. "Oh, uh, I just mean I normally see the same guy coming and going. Any word on him?"

Looking skeptically at Otxoa, the Ertzaina said something into his radio before turning back to him. "Look, you have to step back now. I don't have any more information to give you, and you're not authorized to know the details of these operations."

Otxoa furrowed his brow but did as the Ertzaina said. He walked back to where I was waiting. "He said 'operations,' plural. They must have hit multiple locations at once. This had to have been incredibly complex. I wonder if they were able to take down Heriotza?"

I thought about this for a moment. We still didn't know if Ander had survived. "Any way we can get closer?"

Shaking his head, he responded, "I doubt it. It's pretty locked down."

I let out a sigh as I pulled out our cell phone. The sun would be rising soon. "Should we call him?"

"It's the only option at this point."

I pulled up Ander's contact info and initiated the call. It went straight to voicemail. "His phone's off."

Otxoa stood there, staring at the aftermath of the chaos. I saw him bite his bottom lip, as he sometimes did when he was in deep thought. Shaking his head, he said, "We can't leave. I can't go back without knowing."

I nodded in agreement. We made our way closer to the crowd of people and began to ask them questions. I approached an older gentleman wearing a traditional Basque beret.

"*Perdone, señor* . . . Did you see what happened?"

"No, I just heard the noise. Been a while since I've seen something like this."

"Have you heard about any casualties?"

He clicked his tongue and shook his head. "Some ETA nonsense, I think. I don't really know more than that."

I sighed and began searching for someone else. Otxoa was already conversing with a woman who looked to be returning from a nightclub. Judging by his demeanor, he wasn't getting anywhere either.

I had to think of something. Could I approach one of the Guardias and drop Martinez's name? They may not know her unless they were a high-ranking officer, though, and even then, they'd probably just deny any knowledge. Or they'd take me into custody and I'd have to explain to her that I was, in fact, planning to get Ander out of the city and that she was, in fact, one step ahead of me all along.

There had to be another way. Otxoa seemed to be finished speaking with the woman and began walking toward me.

"You find anything out?"

I clicked my tongue and shook my head.

Otxoa raised an eyebrow. "Looks like all of these people got here after whatever happened, happened. From what I can piece together, it must have been a pretty stealthy operation. I guess ETA occupied one entire floor of the apartment building, so the rest of the floors were evacuated before commencing the raid. That's when the firefight began. The explosion followed soon after. Still not sure about casualties. That seems to be the one piece of information everyone's lacking."

"Yeah . . . doesn't that seem strange?"

Otxoa shrugged. "Not really. It's not something they'd broadcast. Most of the information these people have could have been surmised by the way things wrapped up. No police casualties, no civilian casualties, so less chaotic. Less messy."

"Hmm. Should we stick around?"

"Yeah, let's hang out a little longer. Maybe we'll learn something."

We spent the next hour and a half trying to learn anything we could. After speaking with numerous bystanders and briefly with a Guardia Civil, we were only able to confirm all the information we had previously learned. We still had no idea what had happened to Ander.

Sunrise was imminent, and we were beyond exhausted. Most of the bystanders from a few hours ago had left but were replaced with new bystanders who, of course, had no new information.

"I'm hungry. I'm tired. I need a shower. Let's head back. We can try and sort this out later. There's nothing else we can do. We should call the Hermanas and let them know."

Otxoa didn't look happy about it, but he nodded in agreement knowing we had run into a brick wall. "Alright. Let's go."

I turned around to head back to the bikes. As I did so,

Otxoa spun me around.

"Look!" he said, pointing toward the building. "They're removing debris. You see what they've got?"

I followed the trajectory of his finger and saw an Ertzaina carrying something out to the street. My eyes went wide as I realized what it was.

The painting of the man and the boy in the boat.

"It can't be. How did that survive the blast?"

Otxoa looked as stunned as I was. "I have no idea. It doesn't make sense. I—"

He cut himself off as he saw what they carried out of the wreckage next.

A body bag. Then another. Then another.

Neither of us could look away. I was certain Otxoa had the same sinking feeling I did. They had killed him. He had done so much to help, but they had killed him. Had he resisted? Had it been a mistake? All we could do was stand there watching in disbelief as they loaded the bags into the back of the van bound for the morgue.

Otxoa shook himself out of it first. "Let's go." He called the Hermanas twice and hung up after the first ring each time, which was our abort code. Noticing that I hadn't moved, he repeated himself. "*Oye*, Elder! *Vámonos!*"

I closed my eyes before I turned around, but I couldn't stop them from welling up. Otxoa looked to be in the same boat. We had failed. Time was up, and we had failed. There was nothing more we could do.

CHAPTER 14

We'd hardly spoken a word to each other in three days. It was our last day in the city before heading to Presidente Gonzalez's house to join the rest of the missionaries who were headed home. Little by little, we had gone about packing our things away. I think, though, that as we did so, we realized how little we cared about our trinkets, clothes, or any of our possessions.

I'd hoped to bring something substantial home with me. Something of value. Instead, I just kept losing people. People whose value greatly outweighed my own.

I spent a lot of time thinking about what I'd do when I got home. Would I come back, like I thought I would? Would I stay home, go to school, get a job, start a family? Or would I just keep chasing a dragon that could never be caught?

Then I thought about Otxoa. I'd be able to put thousands of miles between myself and here, but he'd be down the road, about eighty miles away. He could head south and stay with his parents, but I didn't get the sense he planned to do so.

I walked into the living room and admired the Basque flag

that adorned our wall. The red, white, and green color scheme, which for decades had been prohibited from display, represented both the best and the worst of what Euskadi had to offer.

Otxoa walked in and joined me in admiring the flag. "Thinking about the end?"

I shot him a quick, corner-of-the-eye glance. "Something like that."

"It's beautiful, isn't it?"

"In a bittersweet way, yes."

After a moment of silent contemplation, he shook his head and spoke. "What were we thinking?" He sat down at the table in our living room. With a more serious tone, he said, "What if we'd said 'no' to Martinez? What if we'd never met Ander? What if we'd never been assigned to this city? What if it were two other missionaries who may or may not have stopped by Kemina's bakery enough times to really get to know her? What if we hadn't been there when the bomb went off? I could go on and on, but the point is, we *were* there. We *were* assigned to this city. We *did* get to know an amazing human being, and I believe we *did* help Ander, even if it was only to help him find some small measure of peace."

I wasn't in the mood for this. "What's your point?"

"My point is, we can choose to see these last ten weeks as bittersweet, like you said. Or we can choose to accept that it's been something else, something meaningful, and that she wouldn't have wanted us to remember her nor our time here as, like you also put it, anything but one hell of an adventure."

I sat down at the table. "So, that's it? It's that simple?"

"Yeah, man. But don't think it's because I don't care. It's

because thinking about the end is just that. An end. And I . . . *we're* sure as hell not done living. *¿De acuerdo?*"

I sighed, knowing he was right. Accepting it, though, seemed like taking the easy way out. I was carrying Ander's death on my shoulders to satisfy some misplaced sense of self-importance, as if Kemina had entrusted his life to me. It wasn't that Otxoa didn't feel the same way. He had just chosen to accept it and move on.

He stood up, removed the flag from the wall, and neatly folded it before handing it to me. "So, what do you say?"

Placing the flag in my suitcase, I closed it up and cracked another half-smile. "Intermission's over. Time for act two."

EPILOGUE

Maduro was right. The painting was incredible.

I was fortunate to arrive at a time when just a handful of people in the Museo Reina Sofía had stopped to look at Picasso's masterpiece. Most of them continued walking to the next exhibit after lingering for a moment, but I casually snuck a peek at each one to gauge their reaction, which ranged from dislike to indifference, to, at most, moderate curiosity. I shook my head disapprovingly.

I dropped the pamphlet they'd given me upon arrival and, before picking it up, I instinctively put my hand up to where my front pocket would normally have been to make sure my daily planner and pass-along cards didn't fall out. It felt strange to be without my white shirt, tie, and name tag because I was now able to blend in and avoid the looks, laughs, and whispers. What was even stranger, though, was how much I actually missed them.

Studying the section of the painting portraying the grieving woman, I couldn't help but substitute the woman for myself, or Otxoa, or Ander, or Kemina, or so many others.

I reached up to my neck to feel the pendant of St. Ignacio I had received in the mail. As much as Otxoa and I disliked Martinez, she was at least gracious enough to appreciate how much we had invested in her operation to salvage it and send it to me.

One of the museum employees came over to where I was standing to let me know that the museum would be closing in fifteen minutes. I turned back to the painting to take in as much as I could before I left. Tomorrow I'd be taking the train up north; Otxoa still owed me a tour of San Sebastián.

I pulled out my phone to check the time, and as I put it back in my pocket, I felt someone approach me from behind.

"Time to leave, Elder?"

I looked over to see none other than Capitana Martinez standing next to me, looking a bit more casual than the last time we had spoken. "No, not Elder anymore. Are you following me, Capitana?"

"No, not Capitana anymore. Comandante," she said, correcting me.

"Congratulations. I'm glad someone benefited from all our hard work."

"Hmm. You think you were the only ones to put in the work?"

"I think we were the only ones to get worked over."

She seemed to ponder that for a moment. "Did you ever consider the possibility that your feelings weren't our first priority? Did you consider, maybe, that our goal is and always has been to reduce the amount of tragedies, senseless deaths, and weeping mothers and fathers as possible?"

There was so much I wanted to say, but I didn't feel it was

the time or the place.

No, forget that. It *was* the time, and this *was* the place.

"Killing him didn't prevent a tragedy. Killing him didn't reduce the number of senseless deaths. And the only reason it didn't reduce the number of weeping mothers and fathers is because his were already gone. So, tell me, Comandante, what are your priorities, really?"

Martinez ignored the question and nodded toward the painting. "You have good taste. I'll give you that." She looked down at the pendant. Smiling and chuckling, she said, "*Puro Vasco.*"

My heart leapt as I slowly shifted my gaze back her way. She watched the emotions wash over my face, one after another. Surprise, anger, sadness, confusion. Everything finally fell into place.

"You missed something," I said. "The painting of the man and the boy on the boat."

She pursed her lips as if debating whether or not to continue the conversation. "What about it?"

"We were there. We saw them carry it out of the building. It hadn't been damaged." Martinez didn't say anything. "You staged it. You got him out." She remained silent. I positioned myself in front of her. "No one was killed. There were no bodies in those bags."

As hard as she tried, she couldn't keep a smile from forming at the corner of her mouth. "Continue."

"That building wasn't the target. But you had to make it look that way. The real targets were in different locations. The Ertzaina said 'operations.' " She was smiling now, eyebrows raised. "But why blow it up?"

Finally, she indulged me. "Just a controlled demolition. The building was scheduled to be torn down anyway."

"That's why you chose it for his safe house. This had been in the works for weeks. Does Otxoa know?"

"I figured I'd let you tell him. I don't think he's keen on seeing me for a while, if ever again."

"Did you get her? Did you get Heriotza?"

She grimaced. "We didn't. We did, however, round up a handful of her lieutenants. I'm not sure yet how she slipped away. It's possible she was tipped off. But don't worry. She can't hide forever. And who knows? Plenty of missionaries. Maybe we'll recruit the female missionaries next time. They blend in better. They're the smart ones, I think."

I was dumbfounded. We had been played so easily. I touched the pendant. "But why would you send this to me when you knew we thought he was dead?"

"I was against it. But *he* insisted. Said he didn't need it anymore now that he knew where to find what he'd been looking for. Said you'd know what that meant."

And there it was. I nodded in understanding as I asked, "How long have you known where his dad was?"

"We located him shortly after the operation began. Ander had made it a condition of his cooperation with us that we locate him, but we didn't tell Ander where he was until the operation had wrapped up. Tell me, do you know of a place called Ceuta?"

"Yeah. It's a Spanish exclave in Morocco. Why?"

"Do I have to spell it out?"

So many of the feelings of dread and uneasiness I'd had for so long simply vanished. We hadn't failed after all. I looked her in the eye. "Why are you telling me this?"

She took a deep breath and shrugged her shoulders. "Maybe it's because Kemina would have wanted it. Maybe it's because the kid grew on me. Maybe it's because I'd like the Guardia Civil to look like the good guys once in a while."

Before leaving, she pulled out a business card and handed it to me. "In case you ever need a favor. You've sure as hell earned it." Smiling, she nodded and turned to walk away.

"Martinez."

"Yeah?"

"*Eskerrik asko* (thank you)."

She laughed. "Hombre, I have no idea what you're talking about."

As his boat approached the African coastline, Ander looked back to turn his attention to the Iberian Peninsula one last time before looking again toward his destination. The cool wind blew his hair back. The salty seawater peppered his face. But as the coastline grew, so did his excitement.

And so he smiled.

ABOUT THE AUTHOR

Dan Stevens was born in San Diego, California, to two wonderful parents, joined soon after by an amazing younger sister. He spent his childhood involved in sports, drumming, and frequent trips to the movies. After leaving for Spain in 2008 and spending two years falling in love with the country, he returned home and moved to Utah. Dan received his Bachelor's Degree in Spanish from Weber State University in 2013. Two beautiful daughters, Jane and Kate, were born in 2014 and 2017, respectively. He and his daughters still reside in Utah, where they enjoy spending as much time together as possible.